KEVIN'S COUSINS

Martin Riley

BBC BOOKS

For Marie and Joe, my mum and dad

ACKNOWLEDGEMENTS

This book owes much to the inspiration of Yorkshire Wood-craft of Selby, that is my brother, Kevin Riley, master carpenter, cabinet-maker and designer, who makes beautiful wardrobes, dressers and other bespoke furniture, and his wife, Anne Riley, pottery maker, accountant, and craftswoman.

Thanks also to Dave Griffiths for the kick-start, to my editors, Sarah Hoggett and Susan Martineau, to Joe Edmondson and all the other kids who told me the truth about their secret doings and dens, to Angela Beeching and John Smith for their excellent advice, to Ruby and Julie, and to all my family and friends for their love and support.

Published by BBC Books,
a division of BBC Enterprises Limited,
Woodlands, 80 Wood Lane, London W12 0TT
First published 1992
© Martin Riley 1992
ISBN 0 563 36256 1
Set in Times Roman by Goodfellow & Egan, Cambridge
Printed and bound in Great Britain by Clays Ltd, St Ives PLC
Cover printed by Clays Ltd, St Ives PLC

Chapter One

"Good game, Kev!"

"Yeah!"

The last wild day of the summer term had bitten the dust, and from the golden crown of his tough-guy no-frills pudding-basin haircut to the performance soles of his extra high tech Mobilium Sportsters, Kevin Polly felt good to be alive.

It's true his designer labelled trainer tongues only stuck out a pitiful six and a quarter inches; but what was that to Kevin when he'd just whacked the last American softball of the season onto the school roof, watched it roll down, and then – unbelievably – caught it himself!

Kevin Polly knew how to go out in style!

"Milo" Marlow, Kevin's slightly stout but rock-solid best mate, was at his right hand as always. Brian, Milo's mad bad and dangerous little brother, bounced about all over the place as he swiped imaginary balls with imaginary bats over the roofs of imaginary stadiums. He looked like a ballet dancer with fleas – but that was average for Brian.

Kevin took a few more compliments about the game from his mates and said his goodbyes. They weren't long-term goodbyes because Joe, Shebaz and Nick were all in Kevin's gang – a very select gang.

"See you over my house tomorrow!" And then

they swung onto their mountain bikes and cycled off in top Shimano gear along the totally flat road.

"Seeya, Kev!"

"Seeya!"

"Boat Boys Rule!"

Kevin gave them a superstar-type wave. Milo gave them the thumbs-up. Brian stopped bouncing and let out his own wild and woolly whoop of farewell from under his double-quilted anorak!

"Yo! Boat Boys Rule, OK!"

Ian, yet another mate of Kev's, had been standing with the girls – an odd thing to do in Kevin's opinion, but then it *was* the last day of term.

"It's the name of our gang," he explained to Liz and Suzi, two well-known whinge-pots.

"Sounds weird," said Suzi.

"Don't you mean 'Boot Boys'?" said Liz.

"I mean *Boat* Boys! We meet in Kev's dad's workshop by the canal."

The other girl, Tessa Mason, seemed to know all about it already. "It's got an old boat in it!"

Kevin heard this, and felt a dagger of suspicion twist in his brain. What was some girl doing with information like that?

Ian walked slowly up to him – too cool and casual to be believed. Suzi, Liz and Tessa stood together, quietly watchful, as though waiting for something momentous to happen.

"Seeya Saturday, then!"

"Yeah."

"OK if I bring a mate?"

There seemed to be no mate in sight but Ian nodded his head back in the direction of Tessa and the whinge-pots. Something momentous had indeed happened. Kevin flushed and swallowed.

"A girl?!"

"Why not?"

"You know how girls are!"

"I dunno. How *are* they?"

Milo moved nearer. Brian stopped fooling about and turned the radar dish of his anorak hood so as to pick up every word.

Kevin couldn't figure it out. Ian couldn't be really that dumb as to not know what was wrong with girls. It was time to lay it on the line. "You can't have a laugh with them – can you!" he explained. "They're always moanin' an' runnin' home to their mums!"

"Not all girls, Kev," said Milo gently.

Kevin flushed. Both his ears turned pink at what they were hearing.

"Yeah – Tessa's not like that," said Ian.

It was too much.

It was more than too much for Brian who started bouncing about again, pointing and jeering. "Tessa! Tessa Mason!"

Tessa scowled at this and started to walk over to the boys. She had the kind of face that shone like the sunshine when she was happy but right now it looked like gale force ten and rising.

Brian pushed his luck as usual. "Tessa Mason! – She wears Pampers, her!"

And then hurricane Tessa hit him, grabbing his collar and pulling it as far up as his nose. "Shut yer mouth Brian, or I'll shut it for you!"

Brian shut it himself.

Milo, impressed with Tessa's performance on his

brother and fascinated by Ian's daring, chanced his arm with a question. "Are you his *girl* friend?"

Tessa sighed with exasperation but decided not to strike twice. "I'm his *friend*."

"Oh yeah – I remember!" exclaimed Kevin, whose wits were just recovering from the shock of it all. "You used to play kiss chase with him in infant school!"

Brian, delighted, ran out of arms' reach and started a repeated chant like the little stuck record he was. "He loves her! He loves her! He loves her!" followed by disgusting smoochy kissy noises.

Ian wilted with embarrassment. Tessa whirled on Kevin who was smirking triumphantly. "All right then, Kevin Polly – stuff yer stupid Boat Boys!" and then spun off leaving Ian to make his own decision.

Ian didn't hesitate. "Yeah – that goes for me an' all!" he blurted out and ran off after Tessa.

Kevin couldn't believe it! "Oi! Ian!" he called. But it was too late. Ian never even looked back. Tessa's final judgment, on the other hand, was loud enough for Kevin, Milo, Brian and the whole street to hear. "Stupid kids! About time they grew up!"

Kevin, Milo and Brian stood like silent lemons for a moment as they racked their brains for a suitably witty and crushing reply. Brian recovered first. "You big wet sissies!" he shouted. But they were already round the corner and out of sight.

Milo didn't like stupid squabbles. He was ready for compromise. "Let her in, Kev."

Kevin stuck to his principles. "It's the Boat *Boys*, Milo – not the Boat *Girls*!"

"There's even girls in the Boy Scouts these days."

"Well, we're not *in* the Boy Scouts, are we? If I

want to go camping with girls I'll go an' join the Girl Guides."

The very thought of it was too much for Brian. "Yeeeeuch! I'm not goin' camping with no guuurrls!"

A perfect day had turned to three-week-old rhubarb yogurt. A Boat Boy of good standing had deserted the gang for a member of the alien sex. But some things never changed: there was always Brian to take it out on. Kevin pulled Brian's horrible anorak down over his eyes and twirled him round.

"Don't upset yerself Brian! We're goin' home!"

Kevin and Milo raced off down the road leaving Brian to find his head and his balance and work out which way he was pointing.

Chris Polly (Master Carpenter and father of Kevin Polly – American Softball Champion, Boat Boy and Girl-Phobic) was sitting at the kitchen table in his overalls, eating a fat and overflowing cheese and pickle sandwich and drawing scrappy drawings on scrappy paper with the stubby chewed remains of a woodwork pencil.

As he munched and scribbled, his wife Lynda (Canalside Teashop Manager, Hire-boat Cleaner, Carpenter's Accountant and Kevin's mother) looked around for a lost screw. It belonged in the sign that said "Lock Keeper's Cottage. Teas and Snacks" that was supposed to be self-standing but kept falling over. She'd been looking for ten minutes – but finding anything like that in the Polly kitchen needed half a day and a metal detector.

Kevin and his parents lived beside the canal in an

old lock keeper's cottage. It only had one large room downstairs and this room, commonly called the kitchen, was also used as the dining room, the parlour, the laundry, the office, the store-room, the tea and teacake factory for Lynda's garden teas for tourists and the design centre for Chris's carpentry business.

In other words it was a tip, and there were at least a hundred horrible places a screw might have rolled. Lynda had already picked through the dirty washing, heaved up the armchairs, and peered disgustedly at all sorts of gremlin droppings under the cooker. She had now arrived at the stroppy stage.

She snatched up Chris's papers to see if he was hiding the missing screw under them and managed to drop one of them in the butter.

"Oi! Lynda!"

"I've got a screw missin'!" She saw the beginning of a smile on Chris's face. "And I don't want any jokes about it!"

"Who's laughing? That's my new line in luxury wardrobes you're dippin' in the cowgrease!"

"So what's the Furniture Business doing on the kitchen table?"

There was no answer to that, except that in the Polly household everything ended up there eventually. Chris put an arm round Lynda and gave her what he thought was a witty and romantic explanation. "It's cuddlin' up to the Caterin' Business!"

Lynda wasn't ready to be deflected. "Give up, will you, and help me find that flamin' screw!"

A few minutes later both Chris and Lynda were on their hands and knees under the table. Lynda hadn't found what she was looking for but she'd found the root cause of all her problems.

"Marvellous, innit! I'm married to a cabinet maker an' I can't get a simple screw put on a frame."

"Well, I'm married to a café, but I still have to make me own sandwiches."

It looked like big trouble, but before it was time to call a marriage guidance counsellor Lynda spotted something glinting by a table leg. "Hey, look at this."

"It's one of them earrings I gave you for your birthday."

"Aww, I thought I'd lost it for ever."

Lynda smiled. Chris smiled at Lynda. Lynda smiled at Chris. Chris put the earring in Lynda's ear. Lynda gave Chris a kiss. Eyes went misty. Hearts went pitter pat. All quarrels were forgotten as they leaned towards each other for another smooch, and then –

"Muuum! – Muuuuuuuum!" The sudden shout of alarm from the front garden stopped them in midsmooch. There was panic in their son's voice. They leapt to their feet!

Well, they *would* have leapt to their feet – but Chris and Lynda had forgotten for the moment exactly where they were. They only remembered when their heads came into high-speed sharp contact with the underneath of the kitchen table.

"Yaaaah!"

"Aaaahh!"

There was a funny side to this, but neither of them could see it at the time.

*   *   *

The Polly front garden came right out onto the towpath by the canal. On the scrap of lawn were three wooden tables with benches at which the tourists could sit and sip their teas. A paint brush lay on one of them, right beside a sticky tin of Superseal Pucrinol, "The stuff that gets to the parts of silly little wooden men that other varnishes don't reach!"

This was the table at which Brian was sitting, making the kind of face you make if you've sat on wet varnish, and shifting his bum off the bench with an "Eeeyuurrh!" sound.

"Our mum'll murder him!" said Milo, worried at the thought of Brian's trousers being sealed and protected against damp and dry rot.

Kevin disagreed. He could see the look on Lynda's face as she swung open the front door, one hand still holding her bruised head. "I think *my* mum'll murder him first!"

Milo saw the danger as Lynda advanced down the path and he quickly jumped to his brother's defence. "It weren't his fault!"

"Yeah. You should have put a 'wet paint' sign on it," said Kevin.

Lynda was puzzled. "What for? I haven't started painting yet."

"What?!"

Kevin and Milo looked surprised but Brian had an evil satisfied grin stretching from ear to ear.

Lynda forgot her bruised brainbox for a moment and started laughing. "He's havin' you on – the cheeky monkey!"

Brian bounded off the bench and danced a jig of triumph in front of Milo and Kevin. "Fooled ya!

Fooled ya!" Milo ran at him. Brian dived behind the bench. Kevin jumped on it. Lynda dipped the brush in varnish and stuck it under Milo's nose. "Nobody move!"

Nobody moved.

"That's better." Kev's mum plonked the handle in Milo's hand. "I'll go and get a couple more brushes. Now you're all on your holidays you might as well do some work!"

All three boys felt a chill of despair at the mention of the famous four-letter word; but just as Milo was remembering that his mum had almost certainly said that he was to come straight home they heard the sound of a boat's hooter in the locks – a very distinctive sound.

"Rooty tooty tooit!"

Kevin, still standing on the table, had the best view. He could see a seventy foot traditional narrowboat with green and red markings just tugging into the top lock.

"It's the *Jezzy Belle*!"

Milo jumped up to join him. "It is! The Captain's back!"

Kevin did his best beseeching look at his mum and even though she felt she was growing a cartoon-type throbbing egg on top of her head she didn't have the heart to say no. "Go on, then!"

Before she had finished speaking Kevin and Milo had sprinted off along the canal. Brian, caught wrong-footed and left behind again, bleated a "Wait for me!" as he ran after them.

They didn't wait.

* * *

The woman the lads knew as the Captain was called Jessica Bell and, because she had nothing in the world to be ashamed of, least of all her name, she had christened the boat on which she had retired to live the *Jezzy Belle* – after herself. Her relatives thought she was eccentric because three years ago, deciding that at sixty she could do exactly what she wanted, she'd sold her shop, bought a narrowboat and set out to explore the canals of England. Jessica didn't give two or three hoots of her hooter what her relatives thought – she was having the time of her life.

She was just about to step ashore, hat on head, windlass in hand, when Kevin dashed up to her with a greeting.

"Captain!"

"Kevin!" She was just as pleased to see her young friend as he was to see her.

Kevin reached out for the windlass. "I'll do that for you!" Quickly he fitted the key of the windlass over the winding gear and began to turn. The paddles slowly lifted. The water began to trickle and then pour in torrents out of the lock gates as the *Jezzy Belle* started on its journey down the hill.

Milo was next to arrive – "Permission to come aboard, Captain?" – followed closely by Brian – "And me – and me!" Milo was given the Captain's hat and the tiller. Brian sat on the cabin top.

As the boat slowly dropped down in the lock Kevin and the Captain had a shouted conversation against the background roar of the gushing water.

"We finished school today, Captain!"

"What – for ever and ever?!"

Kevin wasn't always good at spotting when he

was being teased. "No. Six weeks, two days –" he consulted his watch "– and seventeen hours!"

"Nearly for ever."

"Yeah. Are you mooring up for the summer?"

"Bottom lock as usual!"

The *Jezzy Belle* was well down now. Milo and Brian decided to ride down with the boat to their own house near the bottom locks. "Oi, Kevin! We're goin' down with the Captain. See you tomorrer!"

"Seeya!"

As the boat went down and Milo's head began to vanish from view he raised his hand to the Captain's hat and gave Kevin a last salute.

"Boat Boys Rule, OK!"

Back at Kevin's house, Lynda still hadn't found her missing screw or started varnishing the tables. She was in the middle of a difficult and mysterious telephone conversation to a friend she hadn't seen since her mother's ruby wedding anniversary, when either she or Chris had made some sort of rash promise that was now coming home to roost.

Chris compulsively put together another mega cheese sandwich while Lynda sweated on the phone.

"That's right, Brigitte! – Yes, I know. Molly and Danny – Did we? Really? – Well what about Danny? – Oh right... No. We *do* remember. Well it was a party, wasn't it – we were all a bit..." Lynda threw a look of despair at Chris. Chris slapped the lid on his cheese mountain. "– carried away!"

Lynda put her hand over the mouthpiece. "She's relying on us, Chris!" Chris groaned and took an

13

ogreish bite out of his sandwich. Lynda returned to her conversation. "When?!... Oh – *Did* he?" Chris coughed as a bit of Cheddar tried to escape his teeth by diving down the wrong hole. Lynda turned away from the phone and looked at him accusingly. "She says *you* arranged it!"

Chris couldn't answer back easily. He had cheese in his windpipe and tears in his eyes. He shook his head in frantic denial. He hadn't agreed to anything. He was innocent!

"Brigitte? ... Brigitte!" But Brigitte had hung up. Lynda put the phone on the hook as though it had just bitten her, sat down and looked Chris right in his watering eye.

It was too late to undo what had been done, to unpromise what had been promised. There was only one thing left to decide.

"Who's gonna tell Kevin about this?"

Chapter Two

"Molly?"

Kevin and his parents were having Sunday tea on a portion of the kitchen table temporarily free of books, papers, catalogues, plant pots, old socks and other clutter.

"Who's Molly?"

Kevin was trying to come to terms with a difficult idea made more difficult because Chris and Lynda were taking their time getting to the point.

"Your cousin Molly," said Chris.

"I haven't got a cousin called Molly!" said Kevin.

"You know – Molly Greenwood," said Lynda, even though it was obvious Kevin knew no such thing. "She was always eating pickled onions off a fork – Aunty Brigitte's daughter."

"She used to call you Polly Wolly Doodle," said his father helpfully. Kevin thought his dad must be having waking nightmares from eating too much cheese. Chris gave up and hit the ball right out of his court. "Aunty Brigitte's an old friend of your mother's!"

Lynda gave a smart return. "More a friend of your father's, really! We met up with her again at your Grandma's ruby wedding party!"

Kevin remembered the party all right. "Oh, yeah. It was the pits! All them old hippy records and you two dancin' an' snoggin' in front of everybody."

Chris decided it was time to say what had to be said before there was any more embarrassment. He cleared his throat and put his serious face on. "Look, Kevin … the point is … we said we'd do your Aunty Brigitte a favour."

By now Kevin was deeply suspicious. "What favour?"

In times of crisis Kevin took refuge in his room. It was a safe haven of peace, tranquillity and perfection and it was different from every other room in the house. It was tidy.

The American football and baseball posters were neatly and squarely tacked to the walls. His collection of scale models of jet fighters, star ships and other plastic techno-weaponry hung in battle simulation, suspended from the ceiling by almost invisible wires. All his sports kit was neatly folded in drawers. All his books were neatly lined on his bookshelf. His comics and magazines were neatly stacked in date order in his comic and magazine box. He had his own portable television which was better than the one downstairs, and a games computer on a Chris Polly designed computer desk with swivel chair.

Kevin sat at his Saki-Hiku Gamesmaster now, trying to break into level seven of the Mystery Dungeon of the Warlock of Weird in time to stop the whole planet exploding, and trying to ignore his mum and dad who were standing at his door attempting to change his mind.

"Come on Kev! It's not the end of the world!" said his dad.

"It is," said Kevin grumpily. The mystery had

been revealed. Kevin's cousin Molly, the daughter of his supposed aunt Brigitte whom he couldn't remember, was coming to stay.

"It's just while her mum's away visiting," explained Lynda.

Kevin left the Warlock of Weird to do what he liked with the planet and swivelled round to face his parents. "So why does she have to stay in *my* room? She'll gunge it all up!"

Lynda appealed to logic. "How can you say that? You've never met her."

Logic didn't come into it. "So? And where am I supposed to sleep?"

"The attic."

"The attic! Put *her* in the attic!"

Kevin's mum pointed out that it was a mess in the attic – even more messy than the rest of the house.

"And it's a bit creepy in the dark," said his dad.

"Well that's where you were gonna put me!" retorted Kevin.

"She's a girl," said Chris, by way of pitiful explanation.

Kevin's principles did a sudden about-turn. "So what! They have girls in the Scouts now, you know!"

Lynda couldn't bear to listen to any more garbage. "Listen, you two! It doesn't matter if she's a Girl Scout or a Boy Guide. She's a guest!" This was the voice of authority.

Kevin made a desperate suggestion. "Tell you what – we'll clean the attic up for her! Me and Milo! We'll move all the junk up one end!" His parents looked doubtful. The promises came tumbling out. "We'll get a broom an' knock all the old cobwebs

17

down. We'll clean the windows an' sweep the floor." It was beyond belief. "We will. Honest! I'll even carry her bags up the attic stairs!" Kevin paused to draw breath.

His mum had a quick eye conference with his dad. "Fair enough."

Kevin gave a sigh of relief and returned to the Warlock of Weird. And then, just as his parents were leaving his room, he had a thought. "When's she coming?"

There was an uncomfortable silence followed by a cough and a pathetic attempt to be nonchalant from Chris. "Er – tomorrow probably."

The morning sun shone brightly on the high and grimy windows of the Boat Boys' headquarters and showed up all the stains and muck on them. A few extra-powerful rays managed to fight their way through and spotlight an Aladdin's cave of nautical and mechanical treasures.

The Boat Club was an extension built on the back of Chris Polly's Canalside Woodcraft Workshop, full of things Kevin's dad might need sometime and couldn't bear to throw away. Inside were old car engines, boat engines, a van seat from the Pollys' last van, a workbench, stacks of reclaimed timber, an armchair, a tub of sawdust, sacks of woodshavings – all sorts of bits and pieces of an ex-joinery and ex-vehicle maintenance nature. In pride of place was the Boat itself.

Well, what was left of the boat! Chris had bought the old cabin cruiser for a song when they'd moved there. He'd planned to do it up so that they could all sail off for days together in the summer. That was ten years ago, but it made a great place to sit and dangle your feet over the prow as Kevin and Milo were doing now.

They were in the middle of cross-questioning Joe Mackavoy, the first Boat Boy to arrive for the meeting. He'd come early bearing bad news. Kevin wasn't pleased. "Why didn't you say yesterday – at school?"

"I only found out last night. I've never been with me dad in the truck before. He goes to France an' Holland an' Germany!" Joe's dad was a long-distance hauler and Joe was deserting the Boat Boys – deserting them for a month to ride round foreign countries with his dad. Kevin tried to let him see the error of his ways. "Boat Boys are gonna get an American football team started this summer – an' then we're gonna get the boat fixed and take it down the canal and camp out!"

Joe looked impressed. Kev laid it on thick. "We're gonna have a great time! We're goin' to the seaside an' all, an' we're goin' to an air display, an' we're gonna build dens over the top field and raid 'em!"

It was tempting but it wasn't enough. "Me dad says he might be going to Czechoslovakia this time," said Joe competitively.

"Traitor!" retorted Kevin, thinking to shame him.

But Joe was adamant. "I gotta go."

"What a pity!" said Kevin, in a tone that suggested that if Joe was going to miss out he only had himself to blame. "I've heard it rains a lot in Czechoslovakia."

"That's two down the plughole!" said Milo morosely as Joe left.

"One!" replied Kevin defensively. "I don't count Ian, and there's still Nick and Shebaz to come!"

"So where are they?"

"They'll be here."

The two of them looked at the door, but instead of Shebaz or Nick it was Brian that came through it. He had something urgent to say. "Oi! Kevin – Milo!" but neither of them wanted to hear it.

"Shurrup, Brian!"

The sign was up – at least until the wind blew – the tables were varnished, and Lynda's café was open for business. There was an incredibly noisy holiday family on one table waiting for their tea and snacks while they tried to control their mountains of luggage and three wild children. The Captain, sitting on the next table along reading her copy of *Boats and Boating*, had a vision of them coming towards her at full steam down a narrow stretch of canal, and reached for a comforting sip of her tea. It tasted disgusting.

Inside the kitchen, there was only Chris and chaos. Lynda was missing and Kevin's dad was trying to decipher an order he'd scribbled in his illegible writing with his carpentry pencil. "Two teas; three coffees; forty teacakes and a round of toast. – *Forty* teacakes?" He tried again. "Two coffees; three teas; four teacakes an' – oh no!"

The kettle was whistling its head off, the toast was leaping out of the toaster and the teacakes were on fire. In a panic, Chris turned the kettle off – as if that would do any good – just as Lynda ran in, grabbed the teacakes and threw them in the sink.

"What are you doin'?!"

"I'm burning the house down! Where have you been?"

Lynda put new teacakes under the grill, poured teas and started buttering the toast. "It's Saturday! I've been getting Marlow's Hire Boats ready for customers!"

"No hurry! Half of them are sitting outside waiting for their toasted teacakes."

Marlow's Holiday Boats were run by Milo and Brian's parents. They needed cleaning every Saturday in the season, ready for the next week's hirers – and Lynda needed the extra money. The Pollys always needed extra money. The problem was that there just weren't enough buyers for Chris's beautiful hand finished furniture. "You wait till I finish these wardrobes," he said as he made his retreat from the kitchen. "There must be somebody appreciates quality round here!"

"I do, Mister Polly!" said the Captain, on her way through the door with her cup in her hand. "So how about a quality cup of tea? This one looks like the cat's done it!"

Chris fumbled for an excuse. "Quality tea doesn't go brown. No dust! No additives! No dyes!"

"And no tea either!" said the Captain. "It's all milk and hot water, is this!"

Chris looked in the teapot – "Oops!" – and then started looking round for some tea bags. At the same time the door bell rang. "I'll go!" said the Captain, and went. The last thing Lynda wanted was more customers. "Tell 'em there's been an engine failure – all buns are running ten minutes late!"

*   *   *

21

The Captain opened the door and found herself looking at a young girl with dark brown hair, wide brown eyes and a big pile of light brown luggage that a sweltering cabby was busy unloading onto the front steps. "Hello."

She just stood there, quietly observing the Captain, who observed in her a girl of strong spirit, imagination and an independent mind.

"Looks like you've got a visitor," called the Captain, "and I don't think she's here for the teacakes!"

Milo and Kevin were still sitting on the prow of the Boat Boys' boat waiting for the other Boat Boys to arrive. They were dry-land fishing – a sport which involved trying to hook items off the floor with string and bent wire coathangers.

Kevin had just managed to hook a cracked teapot when Brian, who hadn't said a word for half an hour, decided to speak again. "Kevin..."

Kevin fumbled and the cracked teapot turned into a broken one. Kevin wasn't pleased. "That was a Man-eating Shark for ten points you just lost me!" Brian shut his mouth again. "Well?" said Kevin. "What is it?"

"Nick isn't coming!"

"What! Why didn't you – !!"

"I tried to tell you but you wouldn't listen! His mum says he's not to come over any more 'cos of him gerrin' stuck on the sewage pipe and the Fire Brigade comin' out!"

That was old history. That was last summer when Nick had stayed out in the sun too long and tried to cross a stream on an overhead pipe.

"That was him! That wasn't us!" protested Milo indignantly to the world at large.

"He's a dipstick!" said Kevin. "We're better off without him. Shebaz is more of a laugh."

Milo agreed. "Yeah! Shebaz! Remember that time we stayed at his house!"

"Yeah, and he told us it had a poltergeist an' me an' Shebaz built that ghost disintegrator."

As the very word "ghost" was uttered there came a rap-rapping on the door, right on cue as in the best horror movies. "A poltergeist!" screamed Brian, trying to hype up some horror even though it was broad daylight. But Kevin wasn't expecting the unnatural – he was expecting the only other Boat Boy still supposed to be coming.

"It's Shebaz! I bet it's Shebaz!" he cried as he ran for the door and opened it and looked for all the world as though he had indeed seen a ghost.

In fact he was looking at a very self-assured, wide-eyed, dark-haired girl, wearing an old-fashioned romany frock and a tatty school jacket with the sleeves rolled up, lapels covered in badges, and a fat book shoved in each pocket.

Kevin didn't look about to say anything, so it was up to her. "Are you Kevin?"

It was a fair question. "Yeah."

"I'm Molly."

At that moment all that Kevin had been trying to forget came into his mind – who she was; what she was doing here; what he had promised to do and what he hadn't mentioned to Milo. All these thoughts coming together caused his body to seize up, giving Molly the impression that she was talking to a zombie. She tried again. "Molly – your cousin."

Kevin blathered. "Yeah – I know... I forgot... I mean, I thought you'd be coming later."

By now Milo and Brian were peering over Kevin's shoulder. Brian was astonished. "A guuurl!"

"That's right," said Molly without nastiness but at the same time succeeding in showing Brian to be the simpleton he was. Kevin blushed. Milo didn't know what to say, and Brian looked like he'd swallowed his tongue. Molly looked at the three of them and wondered if they could communicate better if she tried speaking in Martian.

Then Kevin's dad ambled up in his donkey jacket, and presuming that nothing had been said, started introducing Molly all over again. Then he remembered what Kevin had remembered and was hoping his father hadn't remembered. "I thought you and Milo were supposed to be sortin' out the attic."

This was news to Milo. "What???"

"I was gonna tell you," said Kevin lamely, "– nothing to it!" Milo was about to argue that point but Molly interrupted.

"It doesn't matter. I'll do it myself," she said. She really meant it. Nothing she had seen so far of Kevin and Co. had convinced her that their help would make the job any easier.

But it was now a point of honour for Kev. It was important for Molly to know that he was a man of his word. "No! Wait! – *We'll* do it!" Milo didn't like the sound of the word "we". He had a "going home on urgent business" look about him. "It won't be too bad. Shebaz'll help as well," said Kevin hopefully. "He'll be here in a –"

24

"I'm afraid not, Kev," interrupted Chris. "His mum's just been on the phone to say he's got measles!"

Brian groaned. Kevin and Milo shared a forlorn look. The gang were going down like flies.

Outside in the garden café other insects were having a good time. The bees buzzed, the butterflies fluttered by and the gentle peace of summer ruled OK. The wild holiday boating family had bumped off down the cut, a threat to wildlife and fibreglass alike, leaving Lynda and the Captain to sit in the sunshine and share a little conversation. The Captain sipped her tea. "It's still a bit tacky."

Lynda looked worried. "The tea?"

"The varnish."

Lynda tested it with her finger. It was just on the verge of being not quite dry. The Captain saw the worry and changed the subject. "She seems like an interesting girl."

"Molly?" asked Lynda, although she knew it could be nobody else.

"Yes. She reminds me of an old schoolfriend – used to get up in the middle of the night and play her clarinet in the bathroom."

Lynda's mind leapt ahead. "She'd better not!"

The Captain smiled. "She's an original. You can see it in her eyes. Plenty of character."

This sounded ominous to Lynda. She already had one young person with plenty of character in the house and one was enough. "Do you think our Kevin'll get on with her?"

The Captain was utterly confident. "Oh yes – it'll all work out fine. She'll be like a sister to him!"

25

*   *   *

While these summery sunshine-filled thoughts were being expressed in the garden below, an icy wind of hostility was blowing around the door of Kevin's room. Kevin had been giving Molly the quick tour of the house but it had come to a full stop in front of a new-looking notice in red felt tip, pinned to the outside of Kevin's room. Kevin stepped inside the door, but didn't leave it open for Molly. He indicated the sign with a nod.

Molly read it aloud. "Private."

She gave Kevin a searching look. He didn't like those eyes – they seemed to X-ray right through to the doubtful and double-dealing bits of his brain. He coughed and twitched and muttered a lame explanation. "I have to be careful with my things. You know – with Brian about – he's always gungin' stuff up."

Molly's eyes pierced through the layers of lying waffle and came face to face with the ugly spotty truth. "You don't want me to come in."

Kevin blathered. "Well, like it says, it's, er –"

Molly helped him. "Private?"

The slightly mocking smile on her face was too much for him. The boil burst and all the nastiness came out at once. "It's my private room – right! You've got your room, and I've got my room – and you can't come in my room and you can't touch my things unless I say so!"

Molly didn't flinch. "Right then!"

"Right!"

It was a stand off. Neither side moved. They could have been at the door all day but Kevin couldn't take any more of having his brain scoured by those eyes. "Where's the rest of your stuff?"

26

"Outside the front door."

Kevin walked over and looked down through the window to the mountain of luggage piled on the step. When he turned back he had a pained expression on his face, but there was no way he was going to lose this war of nerves. He forced a confident smile. "Right!"

"Ooooo awwwe!"

Milo had been heaving boxes of books from one end of the attic to the other when he heard the unearthly cry coming from the stairwell. Peering down he could see Kevin's bent back as he struggled to haul Molly's huge wooden trunk up the stairs. It seemed to have slipped, but Molly was supporting the other end.

Milo called down. "Are you all right, Kevin?"

"I'm fine!" whimpered Kevin – who had to be fine. "Let go your end, Molly!"

"I don't think I should!"

"I don't think you should either!" Milo called down.

Kevin gritted his teeth. "I said I'd move it for her, and I'm gonna move it!"

Molly sighed, let go of the trunk and stepped out of the way. From the top of the stairs Milo heard an intake of breath, a yell of pain, a series of thuds and bangs and a juddering crash as the trunk found a final resting place on the landing below. He couldn't resist calling sarcastically down to Molly. "Has he moved it then?"

Nearly half an hour later, with Milo's help, the trunk surfaced above stairs.

Apart from being a dumping ground for junk which had been moved from other dumping grounds in Lynda's annual clear-outs, the attic had hardly been touched. It had an old-fashioned dormer window with coloured glass in some of the panes, wooden beams across the roof timbers, and a black iron fireplace with flowers embossed on its sides. In one corner there was a tool box and some ancient lamps, tin bowls and biscuit tins – probably some lock keeper's legacy.

Molly looked around and was enraptured. "It's great! All full of weird antiques and stuff. I read a story once about some kids who found some magic old pottery in an attic."

Molly looked at Kevin and Milo's blank faces. "It's called *The Owl Service*!"

"Oh yeah," said Milo, not wishing to sound stupid even though he'd never heard of it. Kevin said nothing. It was obvious he wouldn't have read any books that a girl might have read.

Molly walked to the window and looked down at the canal. You could see the whole rise of the locks as they climbed up the hill. A heron flapped across from the trees by the reservoir pool. "It's a fantastic view."

Kevin had seen it all before. He tried passing a sneer to Milo behind her back, but she turned just in time to catch it fading from his face and her smile hardened. Kevin didn't like the way she kept catching him out. He pointed to the trunk, looking for a distraction. "What have you got in here, then?"

Molly moved quickly to shift him out of the way before he could open it. She sat on it and gazed at him fiercely. The eyes were blazing like flame throwers now and singeing Kevin's composure. "What's up?"

Molly waited a moment for dramatic effect and then fixed him with another hard stare. "I don't want it gungin' up. It's *private*."

Milo felt suddenly sorry for Kev and put in a plea for him. "He only wants to *look*."

But Kevin wasn't into begging favours from this Warlock from Weird in a frock. "No I don't. It'll be full of Teddy Bears and Barbie Dolls and My Little Ponies."

Kevin and Milo laughed. Molly wasn't dangerous any more. She was just a silly girl with a box full of silly girls' things – and then Molly banged the trunk with her fist and they both jumped at once. "Nobody looks in my trunk! Understand?" She looked at them both with the ferocity of a tiger and they both understood quite clearly. "There's things stupid boys should keep their noses out of – dangerous secret things –" And then, just for Kevin, in words that hung in the air as though written in fresh blood-red felt-tipped pen, "– private things!"

The two boys stood as though hypnotised for what seemed like minutes. Kevin's mind was in turmoil. What kind of witch-beast had his mother invited into his house? What horrors might really be lurking in her battered leather-strapped trunk? After a while some words joined together and sprang to his lips. "When do you think you might be goin' home?"

Chapter Three

"Six weeks!"

Kevin was fuming and fretting and pacing about in the Boat Club as he contemplated the ruination of the summer holidays. His mate Ian had abandoned ship because they wouldn't have a person of the alien sex in the gang, and now Kevin had one of them living in his house – for six weeks!

Milo was laid back on the old van seat, adrift in the ocean of his mind, following a different, but not unrelated, tack. "They're like that, girls. They enjoy makin' a mystery out of everything."

Kevin started on his tenth circuit round the wrecked boat. "Six weeks! She'll be watchin' soppy films when the football's on – an' cryin' in her hanky – an' squirtin' perfume everywhere."

Milo had stopped drifting and come to a stunning conclusion. "She *wants* us to want to know what's in that trunk."

But Kevin was still on an extended flight of tortured fantasy. "She'll be borrowin' my things an' breakin' em – an' when I tell her off she'll lock herself in the bathroom an' scream an' I'll get done for it!"

"I'm not bothered though," exclaimed Milo, who was very bothered indeed. "I don't care what's in it!"

"In what?" asked Kevin, who had just landed and didn't know what Milo was on about.

"In Molly's trunk. She says there's dangerous things in it, and if there's dangerous things in it, then that's dangerous things in *your* house!"

This was salt in the very sore that Kevin had been scratching. "In *our* house!" he lamented.

"In *your* attic!" said Milo forcefully, standing up to make his point.

Kevin came and stood beside him. It was down to the old team, Kevin and his best rock-solid buddy, companion and chum. He put his arm round Milo's shoulders. "There's only two of us left."

"And Brian," said Milo, not wishing to be dishonourable.

Kevin ignored the irrelevancy, and continued in a voice loaded with the kind of significance you find in old Ronald Reagan cowboy movies. "There's only two of us, Milo – but we're still the Boat Boys – and we're gonna find out what's goin' on round here!"

It was later that afternoon that the next devastating phone call came from Brigitte. Lynda had been doing the account books for Chris's cabinet-making when the fatal bell had rung, and the books still lay open on a patch of the kitchen table. Molly was making a cup of tea, but she had been listening to every word.

Molly's mum was getting a bit overheated and Lynda was lying like mad to calm her down. "Not at all, Brigitte. – No, don't worry. I'm sure one more won't make such a big difference. – I'll talk it over with Chris this afternoon. Bye-bye."

As she put the phone down she saw Molly, pausing in mid-pour, and turning her eyes onto full beam "hopeful but patient".

"We'll see what he says," said Lynda, knowing that she had only used Chris as an opportunity to give her more time to think about it. Molly knew that too, and answered her with a smile.

It was accepted between them that they'd let the matter lie. Lynda went back to struggle with the accounting and Molly brought two cups of tea to the table. She gave one to Lynda and sipped hers in silence while Lynda hunted through Chris's scrappy receipts, undated receipts, and altogether missing receipts.

Molly watched sympathetically as Lynda ploughed up and down the same row of figures. "It looks really difficult."

"Yeah."

"What about Uncle Chris?"

Lynda raised an eyebrow. "Your Uncle Chris can tell exactly how much two by four it takes to build a wardrobe, but don't ask him to work out the price of anything!"

Lynda went back to her calculations, and Molly went back to watching and sipping her tea. Behind their backs a small procession passed, first Kevin tip-toeing silently across the room and through the door leading to the attic stairs; then Milo, creeping quietly; then, when they had both passed through, another smaller figure, wearing a "Rambo" headband and carrying a plastic toy "Spaceblaster".

Molly had a sudden inspiration. "The decimal point's in the wrong place."

Lynda looked at where Molly's finger was pointing. "So it is!" she agreed, correcting the error that had stumped her. "You don't miss much, do you?"

The door gave the barest of clicks as the pint-sized "Rambo" closed it behind him.

"Not usually," said Molly.

Kevin placed his Mobilium trainers carefully on one step at a time. A creak could easily give them away and spoil everything. Milo followed, doing his best with his £15.99 tennis shoes. From behind them, ruining their attempt at stealth, came a sound like an army surplus size ten with metal tips grinding a plank of hardboard into matchwood.

Kevin and Milo turned sharply. "Wassat??!!" The pint-sized "Rambo", who had been climbing the stairs backwards as he'd seen it done by the SAS, whirled about to face them with his "Spaceblaster", as he'd seen it done in *Blake's Seven*, and made even more noise. Milo was appalled. "What are you doin' here, Brian?"

"Same as you! I'm a Boat Boy an' all."

"No you're not, Brian – you're a wazzock!"

"What's that make you then?"

Kevin lost patience. "Shurrup!!" he bellowed, making more noise than both of them. He had arrived at the attic door, and he didn't want any mistakes now that they were so close.

He turned the handle. It swung open an inch. "It's open," he exclaimed, dropping his voice to a whisper again.

"What?" asked Brian from below, slightly louder because he hadn't heard him.

"It's open!" hissed Milo impatiently.

Brian hissed back. "Why don't we go in then?"

"Shush!" whispered Kevin down the stairs.

"What?" asked Brian, who still couldn't hear him.

"I heard something!" called Kevin.

"He heard something!" repeated Milo.

"Can I come past?" asked Molly.

Even the exuberant Brian felt a little silly as he moved out of the way, and Milo felt like a four-year-old caught raiding the fridge as he, too, moved aside without a word to let Molly up to her room.

"Thanks, Milo," she said with exaggerated graciousness. Kevin was still standing in front of her door. It was the final test of power, and Kevin looked like he would rather die than give one inch.

"Excuse me, Kevin," she said with all the politeness of an alligator passing through a shoal of fish, "I have to get something out of my trunk."

Kevin moved about two feet. Molly opened the door, entered the attic and closed the door firmly behind her. For a moment the three boys hesitated, and then concertinaed up to the keyhole like the three stooges. Kevin got to it first. Milo danced from one foot to the other. "Can you see anything?"

"Aaagh!" Kevin jumped back from the door clutching his eye.

"What happened?" cried Milo.

"What happened!?" cried Brian.

"She blew through the keyhole!" cried Kevin, and then turned back to the door as he heard a loud creaking sound from inside. "She's opening the trunk!"

Not risking their eyes at the keyhole, they put their ears to the door and heard a succession of strange and wondrous noises, a shuffling, a ratcheting, a warbling, a whistling, a moaning, a clinking-clanking...

With each new noise Kevin, Milo, and Brian became more puzzled. When the final slam came they turned to each other aghast with bogglement, and then had to jump out of the way quickly as Molly darted out, closed the door behind her, started down the stairs, appeared to have second thoughts, turned back, took a key out of her pocket, locked the door, pocketed the key again and, with a challenging grin and eyes that said "Sort that out fat-heads!", clattered away down the stairs.

Kevin looked like he was chewing glass.

Brian looked at his boots. Milo stepped on one of them. "That was all *your* fault!"

Tea that evening was a tense affair. The Pollys' kitchen table had been cleared so that they could all sit round together. The unfortunate result was that Kevin and Molly were able to look daggers at each other across it.

Lynda spooned herself a few more Brussels sprouts since she was the only one who was eating them and asked, in an apparently casual manner, the question of the century. "How are you two getting on?"

"Fine," said Kevin, giving a performance that would have put Laurence Olivier to shame.

"Fine," said Molly, doing an act that wouldn't have disgraced Bette Davis.

Lynda looked anxiously at Molly. "There's so much junk in the attic – I hope there's enough space."

Molly reassured her. "There's tons of room."

Lynda decided the moment had come. It was

time for the business which had been pending since Aunty Brigitte's second devastating phone call.

"Kevin. Me and your dad have been talking. Aunty Brigitte wants to know –"

Kevin interrupted, firmly grasping the wrong end of the stick. "It's OK. She can stay as long as she likes." Nobody was going to accuse Kevin of running away from mortal combat. He fixed Molly with a benign smile last seen on the face of Dracula. "I like having people to stay!"

"I'm glad about that," said his mum. "You see your Aunty Elaine –"

Kevin reeled at the mention of yet another unknown Aunty. "Who's she?"

"She's Brigitte's husband's sister," Lynda explained, "but she's been taken ill, and now Danny's got nowhere to stay either."

Kevin felt a tightness in his throat, unconnected with his mum's roast spuds. "Danny?"

"Danny," said Molly as though that explained everything.

Kevin looked at those deep dark brown eyes and felt a fearful apprehension.

The sun had just dipped down below the horizon, but the back of the *Jezzy Belle* was illuminated by the soft glow of the boat's battery lamp. A cloud of moths clustered round it, butting themselves senseless, as Kevin and Milo held council with the Captain.

Kevin was leaning over the edge of the boat, dropping pebbles one by one into the water, watching the ripples sparkle with reflected light, and thinking about leaving home. He'd just told Milo and the Captain about the latest lodger.

Milo was aghast. "Another one?!"

"Cousin Danny! Me mum's gone to pick him up from the station."

The Captain thought it was quite amusing. "Only a few days ago you had no cousins! Now you've got two!"

Milo saw no end to it. "I expect there'll be three by tomorrow."

Kevin dropped his next to last pebble and turned to face the Captain. "Can I come and live on your boat?"

"No."

Kevin hadn't thought for one moment she'd say yes. That's what he liked about her. You always knew where you were. He dropped his last stone into the canal, and tried to look on the cheerful side. "At least this cousin's a boy."

"Oh yes?!" said the Captain.

Kevin knew exactly what she meant by "Oh yes?!" but he still tried to wriggle out of it.

"You're a woman! Girls are different!"

This cut no ice with the Captain who gave him one of her five-second silent lectures that were all the more devastating for having no words. Milo thought Kevin had suffered enough and tried a distraction.

"What's he like, this Danny?"

Kevin hadn't stayed long enough to find out. He racked his brains for what they were saying before he'd headed off out. "I dunno – tall – plays basketball."

"Nothing like Molly, then."

"I hope not."

And then they heard a padding along the tow-path, a scuffling and a panting like a dog on a hot day. Brian had arrived in a sweat and hurry. He paused a moment by the mooring. "Permission to come aboard, Captain?"

"Permission granted."

Brian stepped on board and then stood fidgeting, as though he was waiting for something. In Brian's case that usually meant that he wanted feeding.

"I expect you'll want some ship's biscuit," said the Captain and bobbed out of sight down into the cabin.

As soon as she'd gone Brian burst into an excited babble. "I've got it! I've got it! I went round to see you only you weren't there – an' she was goin' out with yer mum in the van – an' it was on the table!" Brian fished something metallic and shiny out of his pocket.

Kevin knew at once what it was. "The key to her room!"

"She just left it there – so I picked it up."

Kevin reached for it, but Brian jumped back, holding the key over the water. There was something he wanted to get cleared up before he parted with such a treasure. "Am I a Boat Boy or what?"

It was a high price but Kevin had no doubt it was worth it. "You're a Boat Boy."

Brian placed the key in Kevin's hand just as the Captain reappeared with the biscuits. Quickly and instinctively he shoved it behind his back. All three boys fell silent. The Captain, who was never anybody's fool, passed the biscuits, and demanded to know what all the mystery was about.

"It's this old trunk of Molly's," explained Milo. "She says it's got something secret in it."

"Something spooky," added Brian, "and she won't tell us what it is."

"What do *you* think, Captain?" asked Kevin. "What's she got in it?"

The Captain let Kevin have it with both barrels. "I don't know, Kevin, and I really think that's Molly's business – don't you?"

Kevin grasped the key to Molly's room tightly in his hand behind his back. He knew the Captain's advice was right, but he wasn't sure if he was going to follow it.

The moon shone in through the dormer window and cast a curious eye on Molly's trunk. It was true what Kevin's dad said about the attic: it *was* creepy at night. Molly had started to decorate it, hanging bits of fabric and curtain to make it like a bedouin tent. In the daylight they looked very colourful but now they filled the dark room with more shapes and shadows than usual. When the wind blew down the chimney they rustled and flapped like an annual general meeting of ghosts and bogies.

A footstep from outside. The sound of a key turning slowly in the lock. Then a shuffling noise inside the attic and a panic from Milo on the landing. "What was that?"

"Nothin'!"

"Keep still, Brian!"

"I *am* still!"

The door creaked open. Kevin squirmed cautiously around it and flattened himself to the wall. Brian came in second, with his "Rambo" headband

and "Spaceblaster" at the ready. He looked nervously at the trunk in the moonlight, and backed off into a corner. Milo was last, moving quickly to take up his prearranged position by the light switch. He reached over and flicked it on.

Nothing happened. The wind blew down the chimney again. A cloud crossed the moon. There was a lot of disappointment about the light not working.

From somewhere came a soft warbling. The same noise they had heard before when Molly had locked them out. "Wassat?"

Luckily Kevin had remembered his torch. He threw a pool of light where he thought the sound had come from. It lit up the trunk.

"It's a bird," said Brian.

"It's not."

A whistle from somewhere. Kevin flashed the torch at the window.

"It came from the trunk," said Milo.

"Don't be stupid!"

"She might have a pigeon in it."

"It wouldn't be able to breathe."

"It might have holes in it."

"You'd see 'em!"

"Secret holes!" said Brian, who'd been convinced by Milo's twisted logic.

Kevin was exasperated by all this nonsense. "You don't keep pigeons in boxes!"

"You do," said Milo. "Pigeon boxes."

At this startling revelation somebody moaned, and it wasn't one of the boys. Something clinked, and it wasn't the keys in anyone's pocket. Kevin flashed his torch everywhere, but there was nothing to be seen. Brian started to panic and edge towards the door. "It's a ghost!"

"Gerraway – it's the late-night movie. You can hear it from downstairs," said Kevin, more to convince himself than anyone else, but Milo was also edging towards the door.

"It can't be the late-night movie, Kev. It's only half past nine!"

It looked like the end of another expedition, and then Kevin thought of facing Molly over the breakfast table the next morning, and every morning for six weeks – and something cracked.

"Do you know something – you two sound just like a pair of girls!" The ultimate insult. Brian and Milo froze in mid-retreat. Kevin flashed his torch on the lid of the trunk. "Are we gonna open this thing or not?"

"Yeah!"

"Yeah!"

Milo and Brian were galvanised again for action, but neither of them were going to move first.

"Well, come on then!" said Kevin, and boldly walked over where no boy had gone before. As he knelt down in front of the box of mysteries Brian and Milo joined him on either side.

The breeze blew the clouds away. The moon came out again and shone wanly through the window. "I feel cold. Don't you?" said Brian.

"No!" said Kevin, who'd had enough shilly-shallying for one night. "Anyone that bottles out of this is out of the gang, OK?" Nobody bottled out.

"I'm going to open it now!" All three of them put their hands to the lid. "Ready?" asked Kevin. They nodded. "All together then – Boat Boys Rule, OK!"

On the "OK" they threw open the lid and Kevin shone his torch inside. Now at last they would know the answer to Molly's little mystery. Now they could gaze on the dangerous secret private things that she didn't want boys to see!

There was a moment's awe-struck silence and then Kevin spoke for all of them.

"It's empty!"

It couldn't be! Perhaps there was a secret drawer – a false bottom? Kevin, Milo and Brian peered into its depths hoping to find a clue.

They looked in vain, but just when they were in exactly the right position a generous mixture of flour, egg, muddy water and unspeakable gunge fell onto their heads from the rafter directly overhead.

"Eurghghghghg!"

Not a pretty sound – not a pretty sight. The lights that hadn't been working were working fine now. Someone had put the bulb back in place and someone was having hysterics behind their backs. They spun round and saw Molly doubled over with laughter. Next to her, in much the same state, stood a tall wiry girl in an ice-blue shell suit. She had confident, open features and a wicked grin not unlike Molly's.

Molly pointed at Kevin's red and angry splattered and speechless face. "I told you it was dangerous."

The stranger spoke. "They look a bit gunged-up, don't they?"

"This is my sister, Danny," said Molly.

"Hiya, Kev."

Kevin's mouth opened and shut. "Your *sister*!"

"My sister... your cousin!"

Danny came over, picked up Kevin's wet hand and shook it for him. "Hope you liked our joke."

"Yeah!" said Molly. "Most boys we know – you just can't have a laugh with them!"

Chapter Four

"One thousand and two, one thousand and three, one thousand and four –"

Danny was making another attempt on her personal basketball bouncing record. It stood at one thousand and seventy-four, so she was still quite a way off.

"One thousand and eight, one thousand and nine –"

Danny wasn't very good at being indoors. She was like a caged tiger – there wasn't room enough for her energy. It was the rain that was the problem, summer rain – just as wet and heavy as winter rain but a lot more annoying. There was nothing to do but stay indoors and bounce.

"One thousand and eleven, one thousand and twelve –"

While the rain pounded on the attic roof, and Danny's basketball pounded on the attic floor, her sister Molly lay on her bed and composed a letter. Molly didn't have a problem about being indoors, but she was having a problem with the letter, partly because of the rain, partly because of Danny's record attempt, but mainly because of the difficulty of reassuring their mum that everything was OK, without telling her too many lies.

"One thousand and twenty-four, one thousand and –"

"Here, Danny! Listen to this!"

"– and twenty-six – and twenty-seven –"

"Dear Mum, Danny and me both miss you lots, but we're both very happy staying with Aunty Lynda and Uncle Chris."

"– thirty-one –"

"We've got a lovely big old attic room."

"Triffic! – thirty-four –"

"And we're right near the canal locks."

Danny bounced the ball over to the window, and looked down at the rain lashing into the dark water. "Forty-three, forty-four –"

Molly looked up and found herself talking to her sister's back – something that seemed to happen regularly. "Are you listenin'?"

"Forty-eight – I'm listenin'!"

"Cousin Kevin seemed a bit put out when we first arrived –"

"Fifty-one –"

"– but now I think he's pleased we're here!"

Danny's mouth dropped open. Her basketball received an accidental uncontrolled double-strength off-centre slap on the side and flew off into another corner of the universe, only twenty-two bounces short of a personal best.

"Huh!!" said Danny, which just about covered everything.

"Well, he might be *slightly* pleased," explained Molly, as Danny recovered the ball from one of the attic's junk-piled corners of the universe. "He might feel different about us this morning."

"Oh yeah!" said Danny, without a single spark of faith, "definitely!"

*   *   *

Just downstairs, in his room directly below the attic, Kevin snarled as the basketball started thumping on his ceiling again. He was getting more and more angry and he hadn't been in the best of moods to start with. For one thing it was raining, and for another he had lost something very dear to him.

The inside of Kevin's room was as neat and tidy and ordered as the inside of Kevin's mind. It was the only place in the house where things didn't get lost. Everything was in its place and some places even had labels on them. It was unthinkable that anything could possibly go missing!

He yanked open desk drawers, looked inside them for the third or fourth time and slammed them shut. He crawled under the bed and pulled up the carpet. He emptied his jar of useful items upside down on the floor and searched frantically through them.

"I've looked through here twice already!" he growled. "It should be here! I *always* put it in the jar!"

Kevin hurled the jar onto his bed. He liked to throw things when he was angry, but he didn't like to break them!

Upstairs the basketball bounced into the early hundreds. Outside the rain stopped and the sunshine brought out groups of gongoozlers, a variety of tourist that likes lounging about the towpath and watching canal boats go up and down in locks.

Downstairs in the kitchen Lynda was suddenly having to deal with trayfulls of teas for these thirsty boatwatchers, while at the same time coping with a visit from Lorraine Marlow, Milo and Brian's mother.

Lorraine was a woman of many opinions, and one of them was that all her opinions were of vital interest to everybody. She also had the special gifts of never feeling in the way, or imagining that anyone's opinions could be more important than her own.

Lorraine had brought Brian with her, but she was happy to sit back and ignore him while he scoffed all the chocolate cake in sight. As Brian fed his face, dropping a few crumbs on the way as a treat for the mice, his mother delicately sipped her percolated coffee – "none of that instant, please, Lynda. I can't bear instant coffee" – and exercised her jaw. "Busy?"

"Very!" said Lynda, as she juggled with two red-hot toasted cheeses.

"I expect you get a lot of trade from people who come for our Hire Boats!"

Lorraine was always talking about "Our Hire Boats". The Marlows ran a small fleet of holiday boats but the way Lorraine went on about it you would think it was Hoseasons International.

Lynda wasn't one to let a piece of snobbery lie. "I expect you hire a lot of boats to people who come for our sandwiches!"

Lorraine grimaced into her freshly ground Colombian cappuccino. "Yes – well, never mind all that business talk. I've come here on a family matter."

Lynda's heart sank. "Really?"

"Yes, I have. Now don't misunderstand me, Lynda. Kevin's a well-brought-up child and he's always very polite! It's the rest of the gang I worry about!"

"The Boat Boys?"

"That's what they call themselves. Remember all the trouble we had last year when that Nick Robinson got himself stuck in a sewerage pipe?"

It was the same old story again and again and she always got it wrong. "It was *on* a sewerage pipe!" corrected Lynda. "He was climbing *along* it!"

Mere facts didn't bother Lorraine. "Well, they had to call the Fire Brigade, didn't they? It's the same every summer. Our eldest knows where to draw the line but young Brian here gets completely carried away!"

"That's right," muttered Brian, finding it hard to speak with his hamster-like cheeks full of cake but reaching for another slice all the same. "I take after me dad!"

Lynda was just fantasising about snatching the plate away from Brian and putting the pitiful remains of the cake in his mother's face when Kevin raced into the room and started emptying drawers as if his life depended on it. "Where's me pen???!"

"What pen?" said Lynda as politely as she could under the circumstances.

"Me Red Arrows pen that I got from Farnborough! Has somebody nicked it?"

Lynda breathed deeply and tried to remember all that she had once learned at yoga and relaxation classes. "Your father and I have got our own pens, Kevin," she said in a kindly and logical manner, which would have done credit to Mr Spock.

Kevin hadn't been to the same classes. "It don't

stop you nickin' mine!" he exclaimed with all the paranoid ferocity of a Clingon Warlord.

Lynda picked up a tray and decided she was safer outside with the snackers and gongoozlers. "Lorraine was just saying how polite you were," she told Kevin as she escaped through the door with her toasted cheeses.

Kevin suddenly realised that they had guests. "Mornin', Mrs Marlow! Hello Brian!" – but they didn't stop him from continuing to turn the kitchen upside down. "It's gorra be somewhere!"

Brian's automatic cake-grabbing hand reached out for the final slice of chocolate cake with chocolate icing. "I haven't seen them girls out today!" he said. "I expect they're scared of gerrin' wet!"

"Aaaaah!" Kevin stopped rummaging and let out a cry of pain, rage and sudden realisation before running out of the kitchen and racing back upstairs.

Lorraine had a good nose for sniffing out trouble of any kind. "So how are you coping with the cousins?" she asked Lynda as she ran back in with the empty tray.

Lynda was still full of deep relaxation and positive thought. "Fine! They're like the daughters I never had."

"Oh really? Well, your Kevin doesn't seem so struck on them."

"It's been a bit of a shock for him but I'm sure he'll get over it," said Lynda, glancing at the empty plate in front of Brian and the chocolate stains round his mouth. "He's not used to having to share."

"A hundred and fifty-one, a hundred and –"
  "Where's my pen?!!"

Danny's second record-breaking attempt of the day was thwarted in its early stages as her crazed and maddened cousin Kevin crashed through the door! Danny froze in mid-bounce. The ball dribbled away to hide itself again.

Kevin's eyes scanned the room and came to rest on Molly, who was sitting on her bed with an envelope in one hand and the personal property of Kevin Polly in the other. "You nicked my pen!"

"I didn't!"

"You got it out of my room!"

"I haven't been in your room!"

"You've been goin' through my private things! It was in the jar on my desk!"

"No it wasn't," said Danny, leaning casually back on the windowsill. "It was on top of your vid screen."

Kevin turned on her. "It was *you*!"

"You were out. Molly said she didn't think you'd mind."

Molly jumped off the bed. "I didn't!"

"You did!"

"I didn't! I *told* you how *private* Kevin's room is. It was you who said he wouldn't mind."

Kevin was confused. Whatever game his cousins were playing it didn't seem to include him any more. "Hey!" he interrupted, "the point is it's *my room!*"

Danny turned on him, still smarting from her second thwarted record bounce. "This is *our* room, but you never asked if you could come in!"

Kevin was on the boil with steam coming out of both ears. "That's different! It's my house, isn't it! And that's my special pen!"

Molly's eyes seemed to fill with compassion at this pitiful outburst. She walked over to Kevin and held out the article in question. "It's a very nice pen." And then, with the most innocent voice she could manage: "Why's it got pink butterflies on it?"

Kevin snatched the pen and blew his lid off. "They're not *pink butterflies*! They're *The Red Arrows Jet Plane Flying Display Squadron*!"

Molly laughed. She knew very well what was on his pen, but it was so easy to wind Kevin up that she just couldn't resist it. Danny, on the other hand, looked quite interested. "Did you get it at Farnborough? I went last year. It was great! Did you see the parachute display?"

Kevin lit up. His button had been pressed.

"Yeah! Free fall from twenty thousand feet!"

Danny was with him all the way. "Flyin' on the wind – I'm gonna do that one day!"

"Yeah! Me too!"

Kevin and Danny were nearly two miles high by now, and sky-diving down through the stratosphere. Molly decided to bring them quickly back to earth. "You can jump off the roof if you like, Kevin, but I wanna ask you something first."

Kevin landed with a bump. "What?"

Danny's face warned her against mischief, but Molly wanted to see if the steam would come out of Kevin's ears again. "Can I borrow your pen back for a minute?" she asked with exaggerated politeness. "I forgot to write the postcode."

Kevin didn't boil this time. He went icy cold. For a few seconds there he had forgotten. For a few seconds he had talked with a girl about Farnborough. It was easy with Danny. She was *sensible*, well, almost – but you couldn't trust them – you couldn't trust any of them. He put his special pen in his pocket and left without a word. They were dangerous – very dangerous. Precautions would have to be taken!

Bang! Bang! Bang!

Brian was out. Despite his mother's fears that he would be contaminated by Kevin's doubtful friends, he'd got out. He'd had to work on her all morning, but he was out!

Now the problem was he couldn't get in! Brian was standing outside "The Boat Boys International Headquarters", as etched by Kevin on the door, and nobody would let him in. And being a boy of simple but effective brain, he'd decided that he would just bang on it until they opened it!

Bang! Bang! Bang!

The door finally opened six inches and Milo peered around it. As soon as he saw who was outside he closed it again sharpish. "Clear off, Brian!"

It wasn't that easy. Brian's simple but effective boot had slotted in just in time, and it gave him enough space to get his nose in. "Wassup, Milo?"

"Go away!"

But Brian had managed to get his scrawny little head through now, so it was more difficult for Milo to squeeze him out – especially in view of Brian's star performance as a murder victim, screaming loud enough for the whole world to hear. "Help! Yer squashin' me! Eurgh! Arrgh! Eugh!"

Milo, not wishing to be taken down the station for Grievous Brotherly Harm, let him in, but he couldn't figure out why his mother had relented. "What you been sayin' to our mum?"

"Nuffin' – I told her there was only you an' Kevin left in the gang now – so she said I could come over."

"And?" asked Milo suspiciously.

"And if I gerrin' trouble it's *your* fault!" shouted Brian with delight as he dived past his mug of a brother, somersaulted over the back of an old armchair and landed with a gymnastic flourish on both his feet.

Kevin raised an eyebrow from the large sheet of paper, on which he'd just finished writing in capitals with his Farnborough pen, and said solemnly, "Rule six: 'Any daft muckin' about by Brian and he's out'!"

"What's all that about?" enquired Brian as Kevin walked past him and pinned what he'd been writing to the door.

"The rules, Brian!" said Kevin with a schoolmasterly flourish. "Rule one: 'Boat Boys meet in the Boat Club at the back of Kev's dad's workshop.'"

"That's not a rule," interrupted Milo. "We do that anyway!"

"Well that makes it an easy rule!" snapped Kevin, who was in no mood to be trifled with. "Rule two: 'Boat Boys under ten are called Junior Boat Boys.'"

"Eugh! I doan wanna be a Jooonia!" cried the Junior Boat Boy. Kevin ignored him. The next rule was the important one.

"Rule three! 'No Girls!'" Kevin folded his arms, and stood straight-backed with his feet apart next to his rules. He felt strong. He felt brave. He felt safe.

53

The next second he felt flattened as Danny swung the door open and knocked him flying back against the wall.

Danny, left standing at the open door, realised that something was wrong. "Sorry. Can I come in?"

Nobody said anything so Danny came in anyway. Kevin slid out from behind the door. He'd had the wind taken out of him in more ways than one. "What d'y'want?"

"Nothin'. I was just walking along the canal an' I thought I'd look in." Danny smiled at the boys and started to stroll about the Boat Club.

Kevin and Brian were totally confused. Milo thought it was best to be civil. "This is where we meet up. What d'y'think?"

"Not bad!" said Danny, meaning "All right", meaning "Pretty good!". "Is that your boat?"

"It's Kev's dad's really," said Milo truthfully, "but he's not bothered about it."

"Looks a wreck."

"Yeah. We're gonna do it up soon though – an' then we'll take it down the canal and camp out."

"I'll help if you like."

"Great."

This *glasnost* type behaviour had gone just about far enough for Kevin. "You can't join in unless you're a Boat Boy!" he blurted out.

Danny didn't even twitch. She had come here on an errand of peace and she was not to be put off. "Fair enough! I'll be a Boat Boy."

Kevin panicked. "We're full up!"

Milo deserted to the enemy. "Come on, Kev! There's only us! We could do with a few more members."

54

"No way! Rule three –"

"No girls!" shouted Brian.

Danny turned to Kevin. He wasn't a complete bozo – he was interested in parachuting, after all. There had to be a way to get through to him. "I'm sorry about the pen," she said. "It was just a joke."

But Kevin was not to be mollified – or even dannified. He slammed shut the door to reveal his words from on high written in two-inch capitals.

"The pen's got nothing to do with it. We've never had girls before. It's in the rules!"

"We've never had rules before, neither," quipped the renegade Milo.

"We've never needed 'em before!"

"You just sat and wrote them out on your own."

"So what?"

"You never asked anyone else."

"No girls!" chanted Brian, who had climbed, piratically, onto the boat. "No girls!"

"There you are," said Kevin. "That's a majority!"

Milo disagreed. "He can't vote. 'Rule Two: Brian's a Junior!'"

Kevin didn't care. "Rule seven: I'm the leader!"

"Who says? We've never had a leader before!"

Kevin was mortally offended. "You're supposed to be my mate! You see what happens! You let girls in – they stir everything up an' we all start fighting!"

Danny had heard enough. She started to leave. "Forget it. I don't want to cause any trouble."

Milo raced to the door. "No. Wait a minute!"

He turned to Kevin, who was just standing impassively. "Look Kev, there's no need to get worked up about it. We haven't actually let anyone in yet. We're just talking about it!"

Whatever good this speech of Milo's was meant to do was totally counteracted by the appearance of Molly's face around the door. "Hiya!"

This was the last straw. "Well talk about it between yerselves!" snapped Kevin and walked off into the damp fields to eat worms.

Brian wavered for a moment and then decided to go home for his tea. Milo shrugged his shoulders and sighed. Molly and Danny did the same and laughed. Then they all laughed, and sat about on the van seat and the old chair and talked. It wasn't that difficult. In fact it seemed quite natural. When the girls had gone Milo decided he'd find Kevin and talk some sense into him.

Talking sense didn't come easy to Kevin that day. After a brief but loud conversation with Milo in the middle of a field, which stampeded a herd of cows, Kevin stormed off again on another gut-churning lonely walk.

This time he spiralled around until he found himself at the *Jezzy Belle*. The Captain was polishing her brasses, and Kevin didn't seem very communicative, so she gave him a rag and some Brasso till he decided he had something to say.

Kevin rubbed and polished and grumbled to himself until the worms he had eaten came up for air. "Everybody's against me!"

"Everybody?" asked the Captain, sceptically.

"Apart from Brian," said Kevin despondently. "Even Milo's on *their* side."

The Captain asked if "they" were the girls. Kevin put his yellow burnishing cloth to one side and out came the whole story punctuated with short exclamations from his audience.

"Yeah, Milo an' Danny and Molly – they all had this talk together – and then Milo came and said they should be in the gang."

"Really?"

"Yeah! He said they were all right, an' I said girls were all the same, an' he said they're all different like boys are different."

"Did he now?"

"Yeah. An' I said we wouldn't have any laughs any more 'cos they get upset easy and get the sulks an' he said boys did that as well."

"Is that so?"

"Yeah! An' I said girls weren't as adventurous as boys and he said how did I know 'cos I never gave them a chance!"

"Well I'll be blowed!"

Kevin paused for breath. "That's what Milo says! – What do *you* say?"

"What do I say?"

"Yeah."

The Captain abandoned the brasses, took her hat off, mopped her brow and made herself comfortable. It was going to be a long business. She looked seriously at Kevin. "You really want to know?"

Chapter Five

No one ever discovered what the Captain said to Kevin, but it seemed to have quite a dramatic effect. The next day Molly and Danny were invited into the Boat Club by Kevin, and as he solemnly crossed off the infamous "Rule Three" he announced that he had changed his mind.

Molly wasn't impressed. "And what if we've changed *our* minds! What if we don't wanna be in your borin' gang any more?"

Danny thought Kevin ought to be given a chance. He certainly seemed to be making more sociable noises.

"You're gonna be here all summer so we might as well get along. We always have a great time in the holidays. We have a good laugh –"

Danny was delighted. Milo couldn't believe his ears. Molly wondered if Kevin was feeling all right. But then came the sting in the tail… "– an' I still think girls'd spoil it."

Milo nearly fell off his perch. He'd never heard such a load of two-faced doublethink. "You just told us you'd changed yer mind!"

Molly and Danny didn't say a word. They just stood up and started to walk out. Danny, especially, felt that she'd been a complete fool to trust him, and now he'd made a turkey out of both of them.

Kevin was devastated to see them go. "Hold on!

– I *have* changed me mind! I've changed me mind about givin' you a chance!"

Molly carried on walking. "Big deal!"

Danny hesitated. "What sort of a chance?"

Kevin explained. "A chance to see if you fit in." It sounded like a con to Milo, but Kevin said loads of gangs had tests you had to do before you got in. It wouldn't be a hard test. It would be a laugh. "Here, Milo – remember that time we made those dens over the back fields and spent all day raidin' em!"

Milo remembered. "Yeah, an' Brian fell in a ditch full of nettles and cow pats, an' mum went spare with him. It was great!"

Molly was standing waiting at the door for Danny, but it did sound like it might be a non-boring way of spending a morning.

"So?" asked Danny.

"So we'll do it again," explained Kevin, "with you two – if you're not chicken."

The back fields weren't fields at all. They were a patch of overgrown waste ground, with a copse of bramble-entangled trees rising onto a small hillock at one side, a tatty hedge at the other, and a shallow mucky murky overgrown ditch running along the far end.

Over the years, to Kevin and Milo and the gang, this patch of wilderness had been the Badlands of Colorado, the Planet of the Zaargs, the Lost Valley of the Dinosaurs, and a good place to hide when you were in trouble.

Now it was a battleground for war. Danny, Molly, Kevin and Milo met under a white flag of truce on top of the hill.

Brian, who'd begged to join in as soon as he found out what was going on despite what happened to him the previous year, was proudly holding a nasty snot-coloured toy gremlin, which no doubt he took to bed instead of a teddy bear.

"OK. Here's our mascot!" he announced defiantly. "Greg the Grem!"

Molly, mocking his serious face with a silly one, held a large fluffy rabbit nose to nose with Brian's ugly little pal. "Babs the Bun!"

Milo was checking through the rules of combat. "You gotta build a secret den and that's where you keep your mascot."

"And the other lot have to try and get it before you get theirs!" said Kevin as he made ready to head off into the trees.

Danny wasn't happy with this. "Hold it, Billy Whiz! Sides aren't fair! You've got three."

"Brian don't count," said Kevin quickly.

"I do!" said Brian assertively.

"You can be the ref," Milo told him.

Kevin was deeply dismayed at this suggestion. "You're jokin'!"

"OK then," said Milo, "I'll be ref."

Kevin quickly calculated that if Milo was ref then Brian was his partner. "That's not fair!"

Molly and Danny watched them squabbling like bad-tempered two-year-olds till they were bored with it. "Boys!" exclaimed Molly.

"Are you gonna argue all day," asked Danny sarkily, "or are we gonna get started?"

Brian looked up at his companion-in-arms. "Come on, Kev! Let's go!"

Kevin still looked less than happy as he

remembered Brian's previous best performance, but Brian was a whole year older, iron-hearted and full of cake and confidence. "Don't worry," he assured Kevin, "I'm good at this!"

Both sides had gone to enormous lengths to avoid the others knowing where they were planning to set up their camp. After circling around, double-tracking, back-tracking and hiding in prickly hedges they managed to lose each other completely.

Molly and Danny found themselves in the thick of the copse on a slight slope. Danny wasn't impressed with it. "This is a lousy spot for a den, Molly."

"Plenty of places to hide."

"Plenty of places for *them* to hide! We need a fort on a hill where we can see them attacking."

"Like Chichester, you mean?" asked Molly.

Danny was keen on history. She knew all about ancient fortifications. "Yeah, with a rampart an' a ditch an' a fence –"

"– an' a Roman legion, an' six weeks to build it," added Molly. "We've got to find somewhere safe before they come looking."

"I don't hear you coming up with any bright ideas."

But Molly was gazing up at one of the beech trees, with wide-open but glazed eyes that meant she'd gone off somewhere in her imagination and might not be back for a few minutes. Danny knew there was nothing to be done, so she whistled and kicked leaves till Molly returned.

"Well?" said Danny. "What's the answer?"

Molly was still looking at the tree. "Remember

that story mum used to read us about 'The Magic Faraway Tree'? Sometimes there was a island at the top – floating in the air."

Danny hooted with derision. "That's it, then! We'll build our den on a flying island! Up you go, Babs!" she cried, and threw the fluffy bunny into the air.

"No – that's not the point!" said Molly.

"Well, what is the point?" said Danny.

"The point is, *sometimes* it was there – but *sometimes* it wasn't."

Kevin and Brian had made camp beside an overgrown ditch. The earth was still soggy from the wetter than average summer downpours. Muddy earth was flying in all directions as Brian scraped away with a stick to make a suitable and secret hiding place for Greg the Grem.

Kevin, meanwhile, was laying some rotten branches, old planks from a dead shed and mouldering green stuff carefully over the ditch.

Milo just sat and watched in his official capacity, which was annoying Kevin considerably.

"Are you gonna help us?"

"I'm the ref."

Brian had another name for it. "You're a lousy traitor!"

Kevin didn't want Milo to think he was bothered. "Just keep diggin', Brian! We're gonna beat those girls anyway."

Brian was quite fired up by these boastful battle words. He flung down his spade and stood like John Wayne on a trench top. "Yeah! Let's grab that rabbit!"

Kevin had to pull him back before he ran amok. "Not yet! Come back here! We haven't finished our defences yet. It's all gorra be camouflaged and under cover."

But Brian was already in movieland. "In case they come over in an aeroplane!" he cried, and threw himself around with his arms outstretched "Eeeeeeeow – daka daka daka daka!" He was getting dangerously close to the bridge.

"Just watch it, Maggotbrain! This is a trick bridge," warned Kevin, explaining his plan with all the relish of a Joker or a Shredder. "If they get this far it'll collapse and tip 'em in the ditch."

"Where you ended up last year," Milo reminded his brother, enjoying the memory of Brian's begrimed face.

Brian didn't want reminding. "That's different!" he objected. "I wasn't bothered anyway. Girls *hate* gerrin' mucky!"

Molly and Danny crouched in the shrubbery near the "Faraway Tree". They were both wearing bits of bush in their hair, and they were blackening their faces with mud in the manner made fashionable by Special Services everywhere.

Molly slapped a dollop onto each cheek and rubbed it well in. "It's supposed to be good for your skin, isn't it?"

Danny wasn't sure. "I think that depends how many worms there are in it."

"None," said Molly, pulling Danny's collar, dropping some earth down, and patting her between the shoulder blades. "They're all down your back!"

Danny smiled horribly – "Thanks, Molly," – and squelched a big handful of wet mud into her sister's hair. "Even?"

"Even!"

"Right! Where's the ladder?"

Molly pulled an old wooden decorating ladder out of the undergrowth. It was an important part of the plan, but she resisted the urge to make a cartoon supervillain speech about it.

"Let's go!" whispered Danny, "Operation Far-away Tree!"

Two hunched shapes flitted from tree to tree, darting from cover to cover along the edge of the copse. It was Kevin and Brian on the move. Kevin slipped behind a slim elm and gave a whistle.

A furtive figure joined Kevin behind the elm. Unfortunately it was a very slim elm, and both their backsides stuck out at the sides.

"Gerraway, Brian!"

"You whistled me!"

"Find yer own hide-out!"

Brian gave up and stepped out into the clearing between the trees to discover that he wasn't alone. "Hey! There's Milo."

Kevin gave up and came out as well. "What are you doing here?"

"I'm the ref," insisted Milo. "I have to be every-where."

"You're not supposed to wander about gerrin' in the way. What's that behind you?"

Milo shrugged his shoulders but he didn't move. Brian jumped, hopped and leapt to a conclusion. "He's hiding something for the girls!"

Kevin had come to the same conclusion. It was a bad day if you couldn't trust your best pal not to rat on you. He marched forward, threatening to push Milo out of the way. "Move, Milo! The ref isn't supposed to help people!"

Milo didn't wait to be pushed. He stepped to one side to reveal – "A ladder!" Brian was first to spot the obvious. It looked as if some effort had been made to blend and camouflage it, but there was no way of hiding what it was.

Kevin laughed in derision. "What a give-away! Too scared to climb a tree without a ladder!"

Brian started leaping about like a dog with a cat at bay. "It's their den! It's their den! Are they up there?"

Kevin peered up into the branches. "No, but I'll bet Babs the Bun is." He hesitated for a moment. He'd prepared a booby trap: perhaps the girls had one as well. He tested the ladder against the tree. It seemed solid enough, and the spokes hadn't been sawn through the middle and rubbed with dirt to make them look untampered with. Girls! They just didn't understand tactics! It was rather a high tree but Kevin scuttled up the ladder without mishap and started to search amongst the branches.

Brian, gazing up from the ground, had a worrying thought. "What if they're off after Greg the Grem?!"

It was quite a sensible thought for Brian, but Kevin wasn't worried. "They can't get to our den without falling in the ditch," he called down, "and they'll never think of digging for him anyway."

"No. We wouldn't have – " said Molly, as she appeared from out of a bush, looking a bit like a bush herself, and whisked the ladder away before Brian could blink or Kevin could think.

"– But we will now!" said Danny, who materialised from another clump of undergrowth and ran off in the opposite direction.

"Get the ladder back!" shouted Kevin at Milo, who was dithering about deciding which way to run. Kevin had suddenly realised that the tree he was in was too high for either girls *or* boys to get safely down without a ladder.

Then, just as Brian started to chase after Molly and the ladder, Kevin changed his mind. Milo could get him down off the tree. The important thing was to avoid being beaten by the girls. "No! Come back! Stop Danny before she gets to the den!"

Brian skidded to a halt, managed a three-point turn and roared off in the opposite direction.

Quiet returned to the countryside. Kevin sat on the lowest branch, still ankle-breaking distance from the ground, and called to Milo, who was standing by the tree calmly observing the flow of events. "Give us a hand, Milo."

Milo sadly but firmly shook his head. "No chance."

"Why not?" said the voice in the tree.

"Like you said, Kev. 'The ref isn't supposed to help people'!"

When Brian arrived in a panic and a lather at Greg the Grem's secret hideaway he found mayhem and mystery. The mayhem was Danny, on the far side of the ditch, digging fast and furiously for Greg the Grem. The mystery was that the trick bridge was still intact. Brian's simple but effective brain cell couldn't compute it. "How did you get over there without the bridge collapsing?"

Danny looked up from her excavation. "Very carefully – one step at a time."

"Oh yeah!" said Brian. Kevin had made the bridge too secure. He'd failed to take into account girls' talent for sneaky tiptoeing and sly skullduggery. Well if they could do it, he could do it. He'd soon creep across and rescue the Grem from enemy hands.

Inch by inch Brian edged his way over the bridge, one step at a time. Approximately half-way across he stopped inching and started screaming as the entire structure gave way and tumbled him into the very same ditch as last year. "Aaaaaagh!"

The brambles were the same. The nettles were the same. From the smell of them, the cowpats were probably the same, too.

In the world above ditch level Danny had found what she was digging for. She held him over the ditch and gave him an authentic gremlinish voice. "Heh heh heh – he's done it again!"

As Brian peered out of his hell hole he saw Molly appear beside her with the ladder. She'd doubled back, of course. "One step at a time – *over the ladder*!" she explained as she lowered it into the ditch and stretched her hand down to help him out.

Brian was in a disgusting state of body and a worse state of mind. The hand of a girlish alien being of the opposite sex was reaching down to help him out – and he was going to have to take it!

Chapter Six

It was the morning of the day after the day of the raiding of the dens. Molly and Danny had risen early, scoffed three and a half shredded wheats each, and ran off out with day-glow energy vibes flashing round their bodies. Kevin had crawled down later, neatly nibbled a three point ten second boiled egg and toast and strolled round to call for Milo.

Milo's mum was with Brian in the Pollys' kitchen, sipping another cup of Colombian fine-roast coffee while Brian got his fingers into the packet of sugar-coated crispy-crunchy raisin-stuffed cereal that Kevin's dad liked to comfort himself with in the morning.

Lynda was busy as usual and Lorraine's jaw was working harder than ever. "Now don't get me wrong, I'm sure they're both very well-behaved when they're in the house, and that Molly seemed such a nice quiet girl at first. Our Brian says it was an accident, and perhaps it was, but my children are important to me, and when one of them comes through the door with half the countryside on him, soaked to the skin, clarted with mud and smelling of cow dung – well, something's going very wrong, isn't it?!"

Brian, the victim in question, just sat and sullenly stuffed denatured cereal into his mouth. Lynda was trying to butter scones with frozen butter from the fridge but only succeeding in tearing them to bits. "Yes," she thought, "something is going wrong. Perhaps I should heat the butter or maybe heat the knife?"

Lorraine was just getting into her stride. "It's a lot of responsibility you're taking on with those girls, Lynda. I don't know what their mother's like, but nature comes out you know."

Lynda let this rubbish pass through one ear and out the other, and concentrated on the butter spreading. Brian got his hand right down to the bottom of the cereal packet. Lorraine found herself coming to a point.

"The point is, if Brian's going to end up coming home in a state like that every day I'll have to keep him indoors all summer, won't I?!"

"Awe, muuum!" moaned Brian, spraying particles of half-chewed toasted wheat on the table.

"That'll be nice," said Lynda absent-mindedly.

"Nice??!!" Lorraine blew a fuse. "I don't think you've been listening to me, Lynda!"

Lynda slapped the knife on the table and spoke her mind. "I've been listening to every word, Lorraine. I'm always listening to you – and I think it's a very good idea for you to keep Brian at home." She leaned over and snatched the cereal packet out of Brian's hands. "You might find out what it costs to feed him!"

Kevin Polly, more resolute than joyful, was walking back with Milo along the towpath towards the Boat Club. Milo was enjoying the situation.

"They beat you!"

"They cheated."

"It was a good laugh. It was a laugh on you!"

"It was a laugh," Kevin conceded.

"So Molly an' Danny are in the gang?"

"Yeah – yeah!" said Kevin as casually as possible, "so long as they don't start trying to take over."

As Kevin Polly uttered these fatal words the two friends arrived at their destination. As they turned away from the canal towards the workshop building, they caught a quick glimpse of Kevin's cousins hanging around by the door.

It seemed a bit suspicious because as soon as Molly and Danny saw the boys approaching they ducked round the door and slammed it after them.

Kevin ran over at top speed with Milo following. He pushed the doorhandle, but it was locked. He rattled the handle and knocked impatiently on the door. "Give up, will yer! Lerrus in!"

Meanwhile Milo had arrived. He just stood and stared at the door for a moment while Kevin banged and rattled, and then tapped him on the shoulder. "Hold on a minute, Kev."

Kevin stopped his assaulting and battering and stepped back. "What's goin' on?"

Milo pointed to the Boat Boys notice that had been displayed on the entrance to the club since Kevin was seven years old. Certain alterations had been made. By altering one word wherever it appeared, the meaning had been drastically changed. "Boat Girls International Headquarters," it now read. "Boat Girls Rule, OK."

"Girls!"

"Boys!"

The girls wouldn't let them in till they agreed about the change of name, so the argument had to carry on in a ludicrous fashion through the keyhole.

Kevin was furious. "Listen, Danny – this gang is called 'The Boat Boys' and always has been!"

"That was before you had girls in it!" shouted Danny.

"And that's how it's stayin'," insisted Kevin. "'Cos there's no way me and Milo are callin' ourselves 'Girls'!"

"Well that's just how me and Molly feel about bein' 'Boys'!"

Milo tried the voice of moderation. "Well *you* wanted to be in the gang."

Danny wasn't feeling very moderate. "Yeah – and now we're in, we're changing the name!"

After lunch, after a lot of banging and arguing and shouting, and running backwards and forwards to complain to Kev's mum and dad, after threats and promises, after Kevin had blamed Milo, and Danny and Molly had blamed Kevin, nothing much had changed except that they had been persuaded to talk to each other on the same side of the door.

Milo was still trying for moderation. "Why don't we take a vote on it?"

"We had one this morning," said Molly. "It was two to none for changing the name."

"That was without us!"

"You should have got up earlier!"

"Yes, well we're here now," interjected Kevin. "And now we're gonna change it right back again!"

"You can't," said Molly. "It's two votes against two!"

71

Milo gave up moderation. "Right! I'll go and get my brother!"

Danny didn't think so. "You're bluffing. Brian's not allowed out till he learns to behave."

"Which means we'll never see him again," said Molly.

At that moment Brian's head, wearing extra-dark sunglasses and an old green Cub Scout hat, popped up from under some old canvas on the back of the boat. "I'm not bein' a Boat Girl – not even for five minutes – not even for five seconds – Yeuch!"

Milo was shocked. Danny was right – he *had* been bluffing. "What are *you* doin' here, Brian?"

Brian took off his dark glasses with a flourish. "Spying."

"You're not supposed to be out!"

"I am! Mum says I drive her bonkers in the house – but I have to report back every hour or – " Brian drew his finger across his throat and made a noise to match.

Kevin was thinking fast. "When's yer next deadline, then?"

"Two o'clock."

Kevin checked his watch. "Five minutes! Let's have a vote – quick!" And then he grabbed Brian's hand, held it in the air, raised his own and signalled Milo to do the same. "That's three to one for the 'Boat Boys'!"

"Not quite!" said Molly. And it wasn't quite, because Milo's hand seemed to be half-up – or was it half-down? Milo's brain seemed to be in the same place. "It doesn't have to be the Boat Boys or the Boat Girls. Maybe we should call it 'the Boat Boys and Girls'! Then everybody would be happy!"

Instead of making everybody happy it made everybody feel sick.

"Pathetic!" said Molly.

"Sounds like Nursery School!" said Danny.

Milo took the huff at this. He'd only meant to be helpful. "You think of something better then!"

As soon as he'd uttered this challenge the mood of the meeting changed. Suddenly they were like some newly formed band with no time to play music because after all there is nothing more important or more fun than thinking up a name.

"Floating Boaters!" suggested Danny.

"Something with more punch!" said Kevin. "How about 'Battlin' Mutant Boater Super Heroes'!"

Brian stuck to his guns. "The Boat Gang Boys And No Girls Club!"

"Shurrup, will yer!" said Milo, but Molly was inspired.

"'Boat Gang'! That's all right!"

Even Kevin was impressed. "Yeah! Keep it simple. 'The Boat Gang'!"

"I said that! That was my idea!" interrupted Brian, who was feeling excluded from the new friendly enthusiasm. Molly didn't argue. She just fixed him with her best innocent questioning look and asked, "What's the time, Brian?"

For a moment Brian didn't understand. He shrugged his shoulders and looked at his watch – and then, as he gazed at the little hand and the big hand, he remembered what his mum had said would happen to him if he didn't report back on the hour every hour. His face turned pink and then puce and then pink again, as he raced out of the

73

door as though he had all the gremlins in Gremlintown on his tail.

As they stood together and watched his wild and worried hop, skip and stumble along the path home, the newly named Boat Gang found they had at least one thing in common already: a cruel and insensitive amusement at a shorter and younger person's misfortune.

Chapter Seven

Tap tap tap tap. Bang bang bang!

The workshop had moved into the kitchen again. Kevin's dad was wielding the hammer, while Danny, Molly, Kevin and Milo crowded round the table, giving advice and getting in his way.

They were working on a new "Boat Gang" headquarters sign, something to cover up all the argument about "Boys" and "Girls" that was still scrawled on the Boat Club door. A new name needed a new image, and Molly had drawn a cartoon of a high-speed power boat riding head-on through the surf.

Being a perfectionist she was trying to add a few extra blue waves and avoid getting tacked to the frame by Chris. Chris, being a perfectionist, was trying to persuade them to have it turned into a piece of master carpentry.

"If you came over the workshop we could do this properly with glue and countersunk wood screws."

Kevin, normally a perfectionist himself, was suffering from hyper impatience. "We want it up now. We haven't got time for all that!"

The truth was he wanted it up before he changed his mind again. He was still having trouble with the idea of being in a gang – with girls.

Milo watched with admiration as Molly added the last curl of blue bow wave and a flock of seagulls scattering out of the way. The wreck of an old canal cruiser in the Boat Club was a long way from the wide blue ocean but that didn't seem to matter.

"That's brilliant!" exclaimed Milo.

"Not bad," said Kevin, still suffering from worries about getting infected by creeping girliness. "I think it should have radar and torpedoes!"

Molly looked as if she might torpedo Kevin if he put one mark on her drawing, so Danny quickly changed the subject. "Let's do our names in the corners!"

There were only four pens, and Kevin ended up with the pink one. To some people pink might just be another attractive colour, but to Kevin it was pure girliness.

"Eucchchch! I'm not – "but he never got the chance to say what he wouldn't do before he was interrupted by his mother with a mixed message. "Nice to see you're all friends at last! Now do you mind moving somewhere else? There's some customers out there been asking for you."

These customers were no ordinary customers. They were Tessa and Ian – the girl that Kevin wouldn't let in the Boat Boys and the renegade Boat Boy who'd gone off with her in protest.

Kevin just stood there like a lemon sherbet, leaving Milo to do the introductions.

"This is Ian an' Tessa! An' this is Danny an' Molly – Kev's cousins."

Tessa smiled. "We've heard all about you!"

"Who from?" asked Danny.

"Milo's brother."

"You'll have heard a load of rubbish, then!"

Tessa and Ian agreed. Brian had evidently been

76

running round the neighbourhood shouting the odds about Kevin and Milo having girls in the gang. They had come round to see if there was any truth in it.

Kevin stopped feeling lemonish and started feeling good. It could be a big gang again. He could have his mate Ian back in it. It would be a way of stopping the cousins taking over – and when Shebaz had recovered from the measles, the boys would be in the majority. "We call it the 'Boat Gang' now," he said, implying the changes were all his doing. "You wanna be in it?"

Ian looked at Tessa for a lead, but annoyingly Tessa didn't say "yes" straight away.

"What are you gonna be doing?" she asked.

"Fixin' up the boat," said Milo.

It was what they'd been going to do every summer for six years and Tessa wasn't interested in the very long term. "I meant, what are you doing this afternoon?"

Kevin was flummoxed. "Dunno. Play cricket?"

Ian had a better idea. "Football! There's one here," he said, picking up the ball that Danny carried everywhere, and trying to bounce it off his forehead. "Ouff!"

Danny enlightened him. "It's a basketball!"

Tessa came up with a logical conclusion. "Why don't we play basketball, then?"

Kevin knew why. "It's soft."

"What??" said Danny, thinking it was Kevin's brain that was soft.

"No. It's dead hard!" said Ian, whose forehead was telling him exactly how hard it was.

But Kevin wasn't talking logic, he was talking

panic. Tessa and Ian were making decisions about what they were all doing that afternoon when he hadn't even officially said they were in the gang yet. He wanted to stop the rot before it started. "Basketball's a sissy game."

Tessa saw through him straight away. "I bet he's never played it!"

Danny went further. "I bet he's no good at it!" she cried, as she gave him a jet-rocket chest pass, without any warning.

Kevin surprised and surpassed himself – he caught it. It winded him but he didn't let go. "You wanna bet!" he coughed.

Brian stood on the workbench in the Boat Club, wearing an old crash helmet with a visor. He'd arrived just after his hourly check-in at home, saying he'd rather put up with girls than be left out, so they'd found something useful for him to do.

Brian wasn't sure exactly what it was that he was usefully doing. "Why do I have to wear a crash helmet?"

Danny explained. "It'll stop you getting hurt. Just stand there, and hold your arms like this – in a circle."

"Oh yeah! I get it!" said Tessa.

Brian didn't get it at all. "There's no position like this in basketball!"

"Yes there is," said Tessa. "It's called 'The Basket'!"

"Aw nooooooo!"

Kevin raised a technicality. "Aren't you supposed to have two?"

78

"We could make him run back and forwards," suggested Milo.

Brian made a move to go home early, but Danny threw the ball to him, and made him feel better. "Here y'are Brian – start us with a jump ball!"

Brian instantly lobbed the basketball between Danny and Kev. Kevin leapt for the ball as though his life depended on it. Danny, surprisingly, just watched and waited. Kevin was so pleased that he'd caught it that he stood there hugging it.

"Bounce it! Bounce it!" called Milo urgently. Somehow this broke Kevin's trance, and he started to dribble it, none too skilfully, towards Brian the Human Basket. Tessa ran towards him threateningly.

"Pass it!" shouted Ian.

Kevin passed it, but rather slowly, and the ball met Tessa on the way. Tessa grabbed it out of the air and started to pivot about as Ian and Milo tried to snatch the ball like frantic two-year-olds.

"Shoot!" shouted Molly, and Tessa went for the basket – that is, Tessa herself did, but the ball didn't. The ball went backwards to Danny instead.

Danny could really shift. She was up to the basket before anyone could see what was happening, faking shots all the time and making Kevin jump and leap in front of her.

"Come on, Kev!" The others had stopped and were laughing at his antics. Kevin, as everyone was now beginning to realise, hadn't had much experience of basketball. Fearing that he was being shown up, which he was, he threw himself violently at the ball – just as Danny made a professional-standard jump turn.

Kevin couldn't change his mind. His feet had already left the ground. He bounced off Danny's hard shoulder and onto the deck, where by chance he landed on his back and had a brilliant view of Danny dropping the ball neatly through Brian's encircled arms.

Kevin hauled himself up on one arm, and complained loudly. "Foul! Cheat!"

Danny walked over to him. "Wassup?"

"You hurt?" asked Molly, genuinely concerned. "You all right?"

Kevin didn't hear everyone's concern. He could only hear a ringing in his ears. "She banged into me!"

Danny was shocked at this accusation. "It was accidental!"

"You're not supposed to bang into people. That's not in the rules."

"There's always a bit of accidental contact. It's not a soft game you know!"

"Cheat!"

By now, the others were standing around Kevin and Danny in a circle. Kevin was on his feet and looking flushed and angry. Molly thought she knew what was hurting him. "You just can't face being beaten by a girl!"

It was the truth, but Kevin was in deep now, and started to bluster. "Come off it! Boys are better than girls – that's why they have different teams! We'd have won that point if we'd been playin' a proper game and you hadn't cheated!"

There could be no backing down from a challenge like that. "All right!" said Danny. "We'll have a *proper game*! On a *proper court*! Boys against girls – five a side!"

"And proper baskets!" added Brian the Human Basket, jumping off the workbench. "An' I'm playin' in it!"

Kevin's answer came without having to think. It was his usual answer to a Brian request. "No you're not."

"I play at school," Brian objected. "I played for 2b when we beat 3c!"

"You're not playin', Brian."

"Why not?"

Kevin walked over and looked down his nose at Brian's upturned pleading face. "'Cos you're *too short*!"

Over the next few days Danny and Kevin assembled their teams. Tessa rounded up her two well-known whingey friends, Suzi and Liz, and told them they were playing in a basketball match so they'd better get used to the idea.

They made a right pair. They were both little and pale-skinned, with blond hair and round noses that were always screwed up in disgust or worry at something, and right now it was basketball that was threatening their well-being.

Tessa knew them well, and knew what they needed. One evening Lynda found herself invited up into the attic to meet the team, and respond to the offer of a job.

"They need a coach, that's all," said Tessa, looking hopefully at Lynda. "They need someone like you to encourage them." The way Tessa said "encourage" it sounded like a whip cracking.

"I get a nervous headache if people shout at me," said Suzi.

"You need a star player! That's what you need!" came a voice from one of the dark mysterious extra-dimensional corners of the attic. It was Brian, trying to look cool in a Cub Scout hat and white-rimmed sunglasses. Having been rejected by the boys, he had decided to show them up by offering his immense talents to the other side. He took off his hat and made a bow. "I'm a Wheeler Dealer Stealer! I'm a Mister Top Assister," he said, trying to sound like a Harlem Globetrotter. "You'd stand a lot more chance with me in your team!"

Danny offered him a couple of home truths. "You're a boy an' you're a pain!"

Tessa added an extra one for luck. "An' you're *too short*!"

It was one truth too many for Brian. "Ha!" He thrust his hat back on his head and stomped off in indignation.

"I'm sorry – he brings out the worst in me," said Tessa. Danny got back to the main agenda. "Will you be our coach, Aunty Lynda?"

"I think so," said Lynda, "– so long as I can organise it round work."

"Great!"

"There's just one thing. It's all boys and girls in the same gang now, right? I mean – it's just a friendly match, this – *isn't* it?"

Kevin, Milo and Ian marched along the road with Shebaz between them. He had been dragged from his sick bed and was now being brainwashed into playing for Kevin's team. Shebaz could see clearly over the heads of his three friends, and that seemed to them to be the main qualification for his basketball superiority.

"You're our star," said Ian, encouragingly.

Shebaz didn't seem too convinced. "I've only just got over the measles!"

Milo examined him closely. "Yeah. I can still see a few spots."

Kevin knew better. "They're not spots! They're zits!"

Shebaz wasn't bothered if they were spots or zits, but he was bothered about something else. "Do you lot know that I've never played basketball before?"

Milo frowned. "That could be a slight problem."

Kevin had had enough of all this negative talk. "All right! He's got a few spots an' he's never played basketball before! But he's got something we haven't!"

Milo knew exactly what Kevin was going to say. "He's tall!" he sighed.

Tall as Shebaz was, he still wasn't totally convinced. "I'll need to practise."

"All taken care of!" said Kevin. "We're booked in at the Sports Centre."

Shebaz had another worry too. He hadn't played basketball but he'd seen it on the television and he knew something was missing. "Don't basketball teams have five players?"

Kevin was ready for that one as well. "Relax. That's been taken care of. It's all been taken care of!"

One of the things that hadn't been taken care of was the height of the basket from the ground. After five minutes' concentrated effort, Milo hadn't managed to get the ball through the hoop. "I think this net's been set for Americans," he said mournfully as his eighteenth effort fell short.

Ian was full of helpful advice. "You're supposed to leap right up and pat the ball down into it. I've seen them do it on the telly."

Milo thought he'd need to grow about three feet before he patted anything down into the basket.

"Go on, Shebaz!" said Kevin. "You're nearer to it than we are!"

Shebaz tried a run and a jump. It was a long run, and in the end a very little jump. It really was a very, *very* little jump – he would have knocked over a garden gnome if it had been standing in the way. The other boys looked shocked and disappointed.

"I think you might need to warm up first," Milo suggested tactfully."

"I think he might need a pair of stepladders," said another less sympathetic voice.

It was Danny, who had just walked onto the court followed by the rest of her team. Kevin had a fright. "What are *you* doing here? The match isn't until next week!"

"We're here for a practice," answered Danny, jauntily, and then a very professional-looking character walked in, wearing a red and blue track suit, white basketball boots and a peaked cap, and carrying a whistle.

Kevin looked twice before he realised who it was. "Mum!!"

Lynda heard the note of betrayal in his voice. "They asked me to help them so I'm helping them. If you want me to help you I'll help you too."

"Yeah – but we've got this court booked!"

Lynda hadn't expected that. "You can't have. I phoned and booked it myself this morning."

And then she saw her husband, who'd also just arrived, wearing a "Sport for all" T-shirt, a pair of old football shorts and some well-matured tennis shoes.

"So did I!" said Chris.

The argument that followed was quite ferocious, and Kevin's dad lost it hands down.

In any case the Sports Centre court was too expensive to hire every day and since necessity is the mother of invention Kevin got busy inventing. What he invented was something that, although it was made of metal junk, looked like it might come alive at any moment. It was a sort of robotic version of Brian the Human Basket, made from a bicycle tyre rim, some old fencing, a frame from a baby's push chair and a lot of wire.

While he was strapping it to the prow of the Boat Gang's boat, Ian and Shebaz practised their passing. They still weren't sure how the game was supposed to be played, but Milo had got hold of some back copies of *New Basketball Monthly* and was reading out instructions.

"You can make the practice harder by each person having a ball –"

Ian and Shebaz picked up a basketball each.

"One player makes a chest pass. The other makes a bounce pass back."

They understood that. It was easy to do if you kept it slow.

"This is good drill to learn how to handle pressure passing."

But the pace seemed to get faster of its own accord. Shebaz and Ian panicked and lost control; the basketballs hit each other and bounced off – and Ian and Shebaz hit each other and bounced off as they tried to reach them.

"Do not use it for beginners," read Milo, "as it will result in chaos."

As the two boys picked themselves off the floor, grumbling that Milo should study the magazine properly before using the practice ideas, Kevin announced that he'd finished his robo-basket. "There you are! Try and get the ball in there!"

"What is it?" asked Shebaz.

"Number five – he's alive!" cried Ian.

Kevin was mortified. "Don't laugh! We've got to make do with what we've got."

"Yeah, and what *have* we got?" said Shebaz. "The girls have had all that training on the court and *we* booked it. Your dad didn't put up much of a fight!"

Kevin jumped down from the boat and grabbed one of the basketballs. "It was a tactical retreat."

"What it was," said Shebaz, "was a massacre!"

Kevin ignored him, and made ready to try a shot at his metal wonder-basket. Milo, meanwhile, had one of his attacks of conscience. "Is it fair, though – your dad playing on our side?"

Kevin got his hands behind the ball and made ready to shoot. "Why not? We're playin' to win, aren't we? There's nothing going to get in our way!"

And with that stirring speech he threw the ball full force at his Meccano-type masterpiece of a high-tech basketball net – which collapsed.

Chapter Eight

The day of the Girls v. Boys Basketball "Friendly" was approaching, and basketball fever was everywhere. It had even infected Kevin's mother and father, who were sitting at opposite ends of their fabulously cluttered kitchen table having what they called "a discussion" at full volume.

"You didn't tell me you were helping the boys!" said Lynda, accusingly.

"You didn't tell me you were helping the girls!" replied Chris in the same manner.

"I'm just *helping*," explained Lynda. "I'm not *playing* for them!"

"The lads were one short. There was nobody else!"

"What about Brian?"

"Be fair!" said Chris, who suffered from the same prejudice as his son.

"*You* be fair!" answered Lynda. "You're giving them an advantage!"

"No more than Danny gives the girls. I've never played before and she's practically a professional."

"You've got a longer reach!"

"So what!" said Chris, standing up and leaning across the table.

Lynda changed her tone. "This *is* going to be a friendly match – isn't it, Chris?"

Chris suddenly felt pompous and silly. He came round the table and gave Lynda a hug. "'Course it is!"

Lynda gave him a hug back. "We're getting as bad as Kevin and Danny!"

"It's only a game after all!" said Chris.

Lynda agreed. "The main thing is it's getting them all together."

Chris smiled. Love and peace ruled OK and everything was fine. "Yeah. It doesn't matter who wins."

He wasn't expecting the long hard look that Lynda gave him – or what she said next. "Oh, I think it *does*!"

From the physical activity going on around the locks over the next week it was clear that Lynda was right and it mattered quite a lot who won. Kevin led his team on fitness runs up and down the towpath and up and over the bridge. When they were up they were up, and when they were down they were down, but Kevin's dad was generally only half-way up, struggling along behind them, puffing and blowing, and wondering what he'd let himself in for.

Liz and Suzi were having more or less the same thoughts as they lagged behind on the girls' fitness marathon.

"I've never liked sport, you know. It's all that changing and showering," panted Liz.

"An' I sweat dead easy," said Suzi, "an' then I get a rash."

Liz was utterly sympathetic. "An' the shower floor's always cold."

"An' it gives you verrucas!" said Suzi, having to stop and catch her breath from the worry of it all.

* * *

The boys had arrived in the back field, and found a reasonable patch of nettle-free level ground to do press ups and star jumps. By the time they'd done a few dozen Chris had turned a whiter shade of pale, but Kevin was in charge, and he was allowing no respite. "One and two and one and two! Right! 'Four man passing on the move'!"

Kevin had obviously been studying Milo's *New Basketball Monthly*. This was like rugby football passing along the line, only – because it was basketball – you weren't allowed to run with the ball. You had to take a step and pass directly.

Kevin needed to remind some of them. "Don't run with the ball! It's not rugby, Milo!"

Milo, not used to being shouted at like this, dropped the ball altogether and kicked it forward.

"It's not football either! 'Three-man weave'!"

This meant that whoever was at the front of the line had to peel off and go to the back of the line when he'd passed it. It was exhausting – and Kevin had yet another exercise ready when they looked like they'd had enough.

"Right! 'Two-man passing'!"

But Ian and Shebaz had stopped altogether. One of their number was laying flat out on the ground and they were worried about his state of health. "Here, Kev," said Shebaz. "What's up with your dad?"

Chris raised his head from the damp dewed grass and told them. "One man passing out!"

In another clearing, not far away, the girls were practising their chest and javelin-type basketball passing techniques. Lynda was proving to be just the coach they needed, and she was still cracking her whip-like voice. "Step in the direction of the pass, Tessa! An' don't forget to snap your wrists as you let go!"

She meant a kind of fast flicked straightening of the wrist but Suzi took it the wrong way.

"I'm not snappin' me wrists! I've got weak wrists as it is."

"Yeah, I don't know why I let Tessa talk me into this," complained Liz, "I never do outdoor stuff!"

Lynda saw them wittering and shouted over to them. "Come on, Liz and Suzi! Put some effort into it!"

This was too much for Suzi's delicate sensibilities. "She's giving me a headache. She's just like our old P.E. teacher, her!"

Liz agreed. "Yeah. I hate being shown up, don't you!?"

"Yeah."

From Brian's point of view the likes of Suzi and Liz had nothing to complain about. He would gladly have swapped places with either of them for a chance to play in the match. On top of that, his mum still insisted that he report home every hour.

While the two teams ran up and down, lifting their knees, snapping their wrists, and doing their javelin passes and three-man weaves, Brian sat on the Captain's cabin top and sulked.

The Captain tried to cheer him up. "If the wind blows you'll stay like that!"

"Humph!"

"You can't be in everything, Brian."

"They never let me be in *anything*."

"I'm sure they'd let you help if you asked."

"They'd make me be the basket again!"

"Not necessarily."

"No. I'll probably be the ball next time!"

The Captain didn't think that was likely, but she understood how Brian felt. It was hard enough being the youngest, and now a big deal was being made about him being the shortest as well. She searched around for a way of getting him involved. "Look, it's the match tomorrow. Why don't you get a bucket and sponge and set up as a trainer. There's bound to be bumps and bruises."

But Brian was not to be deflected. "I want to play! I've got real talent."

"Maybe, but you're a bit–" The Captain had to bite her lip, but Brian knew what she had nearly said.

"*Short*! *I'm a bit short*! Not all basketball players are seven foot, you know."

The Captain was one for facing the truth. "That's right, Brian – but they're not all four foot six, either."

Brian thought about this, and then thought about the Captain's idea of being the trainer with the magic sponge. "Maybe I'll get a break! Maybe someone'll twist their knee and I'll be there ready and it'll be my hour of glory!"

"I wouldn't bank on it," said the Captain, showing Brian her watch.

Brian realised his danger. "Six o'clock! Gotta go! Every hour on the hour or else –"

The Captain knew what "or else" meant. "'Night, Brian!" she said as he leapt off the top of the boat and raced along the towpath with his strange hop-skipping style of running fast.

Next afternoon, at a quarter to four, the two opposing teams, minus Suzi and Liz, who were late as usual, met in the Pollys' kitchen before going down the Sports Centre for the final showdown. Lynda was there too, as the girls' official coach, and the Captain had been press-ganged into being the referee. Brian had turned up with a bucket and sponge, and special permission from his mother not to have to report home till six o'clock.

Kevin and Danny faced each other determinedly. "This is it, then," said Kevin.

"This is it!" said Danny.

Overcome by the drama and significance of the moment Kevin held out his hand and said what he thought he ought to say. "I'm sure the best players will win." It was clear from his tone of voice who the best players were.

"They will," agreed Danny, shaking his hand firmly, and making it quite clear from the tone of her voice who those best players *really* were.

Kevin couldn't resist a further dig. "As long as there's no cheating!"

It was a tense moment. It looked as if the argument they were supposed to settle on the basketball court was going to break out in the kitchen, but the Captain had her own say on the matter.

"There won't be *any* cheating at all, unless you want to give away free shots! And I'd like to remind you that anyone committing five fouls, either personal or technical, will be asked to leave the game."

Milo was impressed. "Wow!"

"It's all in the book!" said the Captain, and

showed them the copy she had tucked in her pocket. "I've been rather worried about refereeing such an important match, and since I understand this is slightly different from netball, I may need to look at the rule book from time to time."

There was a laugh at that which broke some of the tension, but just then Suzi arrived breathless at the door and called for Danny. Danny knew something was wrong. "Where's drippy Lizzy?"

Suzi ignored the insult to her friend and gave them the bad news. "She can't come. She's got to go out shopping for her mum."

Danny was flabbergasted. "What?!"

Tessa rolled her sleeves up and walked to the door. "I'll go and get her."

"I wouldn't bother," said Suzi and everyone knew what she meant. Liz had bottled out. She wouldn't be at home now. She'd be in town having cream cake in some shopping precinct.

Danny sat at the table and faced reality. "We can't play without a full team."

Brian dropped his bucket and sponge with a clang and jumped to her side. "I'm ready! – It's me hour of glory!"

He was, of course, completely ignored. Lynda picked up her kit. "Looks like *I'll* have to play. It'll make it fair – with Chris playing for the lads!"

There were grumbles at this, especially from Brian, but the Captain bustled them out before they could start to argue. "Now then, teams – are we all shipshape? Then it's up anchor and away!"

There was always a group of hangers-about at the Sports Centre, looking for an entertaining match to watch, and there had been some gossip locally between friends and parents, so when the two teams walked out from their dressing rooms there was a cheer to welcome them onto the court.

Under the Captain's watchful eye they wasted no time in taking up position with Danny and Kevin facing each other for the first jump ball.

Nearly everyone was showing signs of tension. Kevin was rubbing his hands together and wiping his eyes, Chris deep breathing, Suzi picking her nose, Molly flexing her arms, and Milo making silly faces to try and make Shebaz laugh, who was standing paralysed with terror. Only Danny was totally relaxed and cool, going through her warm-up routine as though it was just a practice.

Before anybody was ready the Captain started the game, and once it had started everything went shockingly fast. Danny stretched for the ball and flicked it back to Molly. Molly froze for a moment in wonderment as she tried to remember what they'd planned she should do with it. Kevin and Shebaz were racing towards her. Tessa was shouting at her.

"Molly!"

The sound of her name unfroze her and she threw the ball at Tessa, who caught it, dribbled it around the bewildered Milo, and up to Kevin's dad. Chris started jumping about to stop Tessa from shooting. Tessa ignored his antics, and bounce-passed under him to Danny who, quite casually, put the ball in the basket.

Stunned silence – it had all happened so quickly – then cheers and dancing about, and glum looks from the boys, and Suzi, still in the position she'd

94

started in, having not moved one inch, still picking her nose, and quite shocked at the speed of everything.

"Wow!"

Danny walked up to Kevin and taunted him. "Not ready? We'll start again if you like."

Kevin stared at her stonily. "Luck!"

That was already too much of a conversation as far as the Captain was concerned. "Less chit chat – more action! Throw-in to the boys!"

The rest of the first half passed in a blur of action and excitement. Shebaz found springs in his soles after all and scored with a terrific leap. Lynda managed a brilliant dribble with the ball right from guard position to the other end of the court, and then had the ball taken off her by Chris, who passed to Kevin, who scored with a well-placed punchy shot at the basket.

It was Kevin's turn to look smug for ten seconds, and then the smile was wiped from his face as Tessa scored from a throw-in by Molly, and Lynda played the same trick on Chris, stealing the ball from him at the last moment and scoring from way back.

From then on the lead passed backwards and forwards, with neither side getting a clear advantage. Finally, with the girls one basket down, Chris tried a long lob down to Kevin who was hovering within striking distance. It looked like it was going to fall short, well within range of Suzi, who was standing twiddling with her hair.

"Suzi!!!" shouted Danny, and Suzi woke up and flailed wildly with one hand towards the falling ball. Somehow she hit it, and somehow it deflected it towards the right basket. For a moment it hung on the lip, and then fell through to cheers from everybody.

The Captain blew the whistle. "Twenty-two – twenty-two! Half-time!"

In the girls' changing room everybody crowded round Suzi, congratulating her.

"What a shot!"

"Brilliant reactions!!"

Danny reached out and shook Suzi's hand. Suzi let out a scream. "Yeow!"

"Careful!" said the Captain. "She's hurt!"

"I am!" said Suzi with that mixture of fear and joy with which a hypochondriac greets the news that they are *really* ill. "It's my wrist! I told you I had a weak wrist!"

The Captain blew her whistle and Brian came running in with his bucket. There wasn't much he could do except apply the magic cool sponge and then wait for Lynda and the Captain to examine her wrist properly.

Lynda could see that it was a serious sprain. "She can't play like this."

Danny was mortified. "What are we gonna do? We can't play one short! We can't let those boys beat us!"

"They can't anyway. They haven't!" said the Captain. "You've already proved your point."

There was general agreement on that score.

The Captain smiled. "It's all been very serious so far. I think it's time for a bit of fun."

When the teams emerged for the second half the Captain made an announcement. "Suzi has sustained a hand injury after scoring the equaliser in the first half, so the girls are playing a substitute."

There was enthusiastic clapping for Suzi and for her substitute from the sidelines, and onto the court walked a very short figure wearing Suzi's red leotard, leg warmers and shorts, as well as a Cub Scout hat and extra dark sunglasses.

Milo couldn't believe his eyes. "Brian!!"

Kevin knew instinctively it was some kind of double-dealing by the girls. "Foul play! You can't do that!"

He was about to point out that a boy couldn't play on the girls' side when Milo whispered in his ear. "Leave it, Kev! He's hopeless! He'll scupper 'em!"

Kevin saw the obvious truth in that and his expression changed. "OK. Let's go!"

The Captain blew the whistle.

And the basketball started being played – real basketball – top-quality, high-tech, no-messing basketball, clever fakes, rolling passes, backward dribbling, swapping hands in mid-run, twists, turns, making shots, scoring shots, and a long run down the centre of the court, beating all opposition and scoring the last basket just as the final whistle sounded.

And all this 'real basketball' was being played by Brian, Brian the Human Basket, who at last had a chance to demonstrate what he'd been telling everyone all along – how 2c had beaten 3b.

* * *

After the last whistle's long blow Danny danced up to Kevin. "We pasted you!"

"Thanks to Shorty here!" added Tessa.

"It was fair and square!" insisted Danny, "and no cheating!"

But Kevin wasn't going to give in. "You did cheat! It was *Boys* against *Girls* an' you played a *boy*! So *we* won!"

Kevin and Danny looked ready for more but Milo didn't feel like starting another feud. "I don't think anybody won."

Molly agreed. "Apart from Brian!"

"Yeah. I think he played better than any of us!" said Lynda, lifting Brian's hand in the air like a champion boxer. "Short people rule, OK!"

"Well done, Brian!" said the Captain, reaching over to pat him on the back.

Brian smiled happily at her. "Is it me hour of glory?"

The Captain gave a nod. "I'd say so."

This is what Brian wanted to hear. He shouted aloud and punched the air with his fist. "Yeahhhh! It's me hour of glor-eeee!"

But then Milo noticed something that his brother hadn't. "It's your hour of *something else*, Brian. Have you seen the time?!"

Brian turned round and looked at the clock on the Sports Centre wall. When he saw the little hand pointing straight down and the big hand pointing straight up, his expression of triumph vanished and shocked horror took its place. "Ah no! Me mum'll kill me!"

There was laughter and applause and expressions of sympathy from everyone. Even Danny and

Kevin shared the joke as Brian spun on his heels and raced through the crowd to the exit.

And then, just as he reached the door, moved by the applause that was following him and not wishing to miss a moment of his hour of glory, even in the face of his mother's anger, he stopped, turned back, whisked off his Cub hat – and bowed low to acknowledge his fans.

Chapter Nine

Milo sat on the edge of Kevin's bed and waited impatiently for Kevin and Danny to finish playing their Dungeons and Dragons video computer game. It was one of those games that could go on for ever, a tense exciting adventure quest, with lots of levels and zero chance of getting to the end.

In the weeks following the basketball match tensions between Kevin and his cousins had eased. The red felt-penned "private" notice had vanished from Kevin's door, and Danny and Molly walked freely into the Kevin Polly no-go area without being accused of "gunging it up".

The "Boat Gang" now had all the original boys apart from Nick who got stuck on the sewage pipe, and Joe who'd gone round Europe in his dad's truck. Of the girls, Tessa was usually about, and Liz and Suzi showed their faces when they weren't shopping or visiting the doctors.

Kevin and Danny seemed to share the leadership between them, although no one had ever discussed it, and despite this they were still fighting each other. They *enjoyed* fighting each other!

That morning, however, they had joined forces to fight fantasy creatures from the dungeons of the Wizard of Weird.

"Look out! Look out!"

"What?!!" said Danny, without taking her eyes from the screen or her fingers from the controls.

"There's a Fourth-Level Double-Headed Zombie Vampire round the next bend."

"I can see it!"

"Vanish it with yer spell, then!"

"I've only got one spell left. I'm gonna race it to the door!"

Milo kicked his heels with boredom. "Don't hurry yourselves," he muttered sarcastically, but they were so absorbed they didn't even hear him.

"You haven't got a key!" shouted Kevin urgently.

"I have!" insisted Danny, but next moment there were grisly noises of defeat and destruction from the flickering screen.

Kevin tried to shift her off his chair. "Go on – move over. I'll show you how it's done."

Danny wouldn't budge. "No. I've got 30 seconds left."

"Go on, then!" said Kevin, hassling her to play.

Milo was getting really fed up. "Go on where? You've been goin' nowhere! You've been sat there for half an hour!"

But Kevin was firmly locked into fantasy land. "Hold on! Just a minute! We gotta get past the Guardian of the Rainbow Bridge!"

Milo wasn't moaning now – he was angry. "You said we were goin' over the fields!"

"We are."

"We are going!" echoed Danny.

Milo poked his head between them. "You know, it was better when you two were enemies."

"We are!" said Danny happily.

"We are enemies!" insisted Kevin.

"Zaaaaaaap – de da de da deee daaa!" While

101

they were looking away the Wizard of Weird had had his evil way. Kevin and Danny weren't too happy.

Kevin jabbed Milo with an accusing finger. "Now look what you've made us do!"

"Me?!!"

And then Danny had an idea. "Come on, Kev. Let's go over the canal bridge an' play it for real."

Kevin was instantly in favour. "Yeah – 'Gettin' past the Guardian'!"

"I'll go and get Molly!" said Danny as she dashed out of the door and ran upstairs.

Milo didn't hold out much hope. "She'll be lucky!"

Molly liked to read. She liked to read in almost any position. One of her favourite positions was to flop over the arm of a chair with the book lying open on the floor. Her mother had told her that this would make the blood run to her head, and she was probably right.

This was the way Molly and her book were arranged when Danny ran into the attic and started putting her boots on. "Come on, Molly. We're goin' out!"

Molly didn't flinch. Reading for her was even more engrossing than video games were for Danny. In any case, one of the effects of the blood running to her head seemed to be that it made her deaf as well.

Danny came and bellowed in her ear. "Molly! Can you hear me?"

If Molly could she made no sign of it. Instead she calmly turned the next page and continued reading.

Danny remembered a trick their mother used on Molly when she needed her attention. "Do you want a five pound note?"

She didn't look round – but she definitely twitched. Danny was delighted. "Hah! Gotcha!"

Molly, now in the land of the living, gripped her book defensively and curled up with it in the armchair. "Get lost!"

"Come on, Molly. Pack in this borin' book. We're goin' over the fields."

"Just let me finish this chapter."

Danny knew from long experience that this was book reader's language for "just a minute" and she knew how long that kind of minute lasted. "Come on, Molly!"

Molly was getting desperate. "Just one more page!"

Danny knew it was now or never. She snatched the book out of Molly's hands and ran down the stairs. Molly ran after her. "Oi! Come back! Bring that book back here!"

Danny reached the bottom of the stairs and shouted back at her "Come and get it!" before running out of the front door and away!

Brian and Shebaz were already over the back fields. They were climbing up the hill, laughing and panting and covered in grass, leaves and bits, when Milo and Kevin arrived, followed by Danny, sprinting along with a book in her hand, followed by Molly shouting for her to come back.

"Danny! Danny!"

Danny threw herself onto the ground near the others and Molly hurled herself at her sister to get the book back. "Give-us it!"

"No! Not till we're finished!"

Shebaz watched all this, brushing the leaves and twigs out of his hair. "Where you lot bin?"

"Waiting for Kev an' Danny!" answered Milo with just a trace of bitterness.

"You're kiddin'!" interjected Kevin. "*We've* been waitin' for *them*!"

Milo folded his arms and sulked. Danny wondered how Shebaz had come to look like a compost heap.

"Falling down the hill," he explained.

"Yeah! Watch this!" whooped Brian, and with a blood-curdling yell he threw himself into the air and rolled, round and around, faster and faster down the slope.

Milo thought he might be going off-course. "Watch out for the nettles!" he called out, but Brian had vanished from sight.

"That's what *we've* been doing," said Shebaz. "What have you lot been doin'?"

"Tryin' to read my book," said Molly petulantly. "I've just got to the bit where the Tyke Tiler climbs onto the school roof and –" Thinking that Danny would be distracted Molly tried to grab the book off her, but didn't succeed.

"No!" Danny said, tucking it down the back of her belt. "If I let you have it you'll just sit here and read it! You gotta play this game first."

"What game?" asked Molly, and then without waiting for a reply, "I don't wanna play any games!"

Milo agreed. "I think I'd rather fall down the hill!" said Milo, as he and Shebaz, giving a pair of eardrum-rattling yells at least the volume of

Brian's, threw themselves down the slope after him.

It took Danny and Kevin over half an hour of cajoling and threatening to get everyone rounded up and where they wanted them to play "The Guardian of the Bridge to the Castle of the Dungeon of the Wizard of Weird".

Danny and Kevin stood the "fields" side of the canal bridge and tried to ignore Brian who, since his "fall" down the hill, had been hopping about more than usual and making noises like the ones you make when you've got a hot potato in your mouth.

"Yah har hoo hore hoo hoo!"

Milo grinned. "I warned you about the nettles!"

"Are you listenin'!" asked Danny, in a way that made it an order rather than a question. "One of us has to be the Guardian of the Bridge."

"The Guardian is a super-strong super-hero," explained Kevin, "with magical mental powers!"

Brian stopped hopping. "That's me, innit?!"

Shebaz laughed. "You've kept that a secret!"

Danny saw that they were getting undisciplined again. "Listen, will you! We don't know who it is yet." And then, after a pause for dramatic effect, she announced, "It's Molly!"

Molly wasn't keen. "I don't wanna be It! I wanna read me book!"

Danny ignored her complaining and moved her by her shoulders so that she was between the gang and the bridge. The others backed off and Kevin explained the rest.

"You're It! You're the Guardian of the Bridge

an' you gotta stop us getting across it to the other side!"

"How?" asked Molly, being deliberately dense.

"You gotta tag us before we get over!"

Now that it was all explained, Danny and Kevin went back to join the others. Kevin counted to three and shouted "Go!", and they all raced for the bridge.

As they ran, Molly ran for the bridge too, and then turned and stood blocking the way like some ancient hero. Everyone else ground to a halt. There was no room to get past without getting tagged.

"Hold on! You can't do that!" shouted Kevin. "You're in the way!"

"I thought that was the idea!" said Molly.

Danny was furious. "Nobody's got a chance of getting past! Stop tryin' to be clever!"

Molly grinned. "I'm usin' me magic mental powers, aren't I?"

"Yeah. That's the game isn't it?" said Milo, who was enjoying the joke.

"*You* be It, Danny!" suggested Molly."You can show us how it's done."

Danny accepted the challenge. "OK. Fair enough! I'm on! I'm not allowed to go back past this stone or forward past the tree – right!"

Kevin gave them the "go" again and they all ran. This time everyone veered to the left of Danny and got past and over the bridge to the fields – apart from Molly who went to the right.

Danny followed her as she ran backwards and forwards, determined that Molly should be tagged, but for a while it was stalemate. Danny couldn't get close enough, and Molly kept backing away.

Then Molly started to look tired and Danny closed in for the kill. Milo could see what was going to happen and called out loudly.

"Here! Danny!"

Danny turned, distracted. It was the moment Molly had been waiting for. She snatched her book out of her sister's belt and ran off back towards the house.

Lynda and Chris were sitting in the kitchen watching television.

It was just another Australian soap opera, with another highly original tale of romance and jealousy and conversations on sofas, but from the way Lynda and Chris were behaving, jumping out of their armchairs and shouting encouragement, you might imagine they were watching American wrestling.

Lynda was on Bryony's side. "Come on, Bryony! You tell him."

Chris was on Tod's side. "It's not his fault!"

Lynda turned on Chris as though he had been Tod himself. "Oh yeah! Well if Bruce hadn't been so suspicious of Bryony she wouldn't have gone to the beach with Brad to make Bruce jealous, and Brad wouldn't have busted up with Bruce's sister Sheila, and Bruce and Bryony wouldn't have come home without the burgers for the barbie!"

There was no arguing with that, and there was no opportunity either as the room was taken over by the real-life argument between Molly, who had just walked into the kitchen, Danny and Kevin, who had followed her, and Milo, who had followed *them*.

Molly was still sticking to her guns. "I'm not comin' back. I'm not – and you can't make me!"

Danny was embarrassed in front of her uncle and aunt. "You're makin' a right fool of yourself!"

Molly didn't care who was listening. She was full of righteousness, "I've had enough of it! You always boss me around!"

"I don't!"

"You do!"

"You do!" said Milo, now clearly on Molly's side.

"She doesn't," said Kevin, showing where his loyalty lay.

There followed an uproarious confusion of "does's" and "doesn'ts" from all sides, until Chris and Lynda could stand no more.

"Be quiet, will you!" bellowed Kevin's dad. "We don't want to listen to your bickering!"

"No," said his mum. "We can't hear the television! If you want to argue, go upstairs!"

And then they settled back to watch the made-up bickering on the television, while the real-life showdown carried on elsewhere.

Danny was climbing up the stairs after Molly. "You've always been the same – ever since we were little!"

Molly clutched the bannister for support and let fly. "*You* have! – Pesterin' me, teasin' me, an' if I hit you back you went runnin' to mum an' I got the blame!"

Milo had every sympathy. "Yeah! Brian does that!"

Danny didn't want to hear about it. "You keep your nose out!"

"See!" said Molly. "She's bossin' you an' all!" And then she pushed open the attic door and flung herself in her chair with her book.

Kevin was getting defensive. "We were just playin' a game. Someone's got to organise it!"

Danny came in to help him out. "Someone's got to suggest doing something or we'd all do nothing."

Kevin took Milo by his arm. "Come on, you two! Come on out!"

Milo resisted. "There you go! Pushing!"

Kevin got technical. "Pulling!" and then tried blackmail. "You're supposed to be my mate, aren't you?!"

That was just the wrong thing to say to Milo at that moment. "That's right. I'm *your mate*," he roared. "You're never *my* mate! 'Who's Milo?' 'Kevin's mate'!"

"Same as me!" chimed Molly, looking up from her book. "I'm *her* sister!"

There was no holding Milo back either now. The worm had turned. He faced Kevin and Danny head on. "You're completely pathetic, you two. You're always fightin' each other, and you're just the same as each other – a right pair of bossyboots!"

"At least we do things!" Kevin spluttered.

Danny turned on Molly, who had her nose deliberately in her book. "Yeah! You're not even *reading* that! You're just *pretending* to read it to wind me up!"

Before Molly realised what was happening Danny snatched the book out of Molly's hands, and ran to the attic window. "It's goin' in the cut!" Danny waved it backwards and forwards as though she was really going to throw it.

Molly's dark eyes blazed and sparked with rage. "If that book goes in the canal I'll never speak to you again."

The café was open, and there were one or two tourists as well as what could be called "the residents". Lorraine and the Captain had been sitting together at the same table when the book had come flying out of the window, followed by Milo and Kevin and his cousins through the door.

Milo and Kevin had joined the Captain, and tried to look as though nothing odd was going on. Molly was trying to fish the book out of the canal with a net. Danny was trying unsuccessfully to explain. "It just slipped."

Molly ignored her and shouted to Kevin and Milo. "Tell her she chucked it!"

Milo shouted back to Danny, "You chucked it!"

Kevin leaned over to Milo. "No she didn't!"

By now several of the tourists were looking askance, and Lorraine was climbing on one of her high horses. "Just what's going on here?", and then severely to her eldest son, "It's very rude to shout like that," and then to the Captain, "It's certainly not a habit he's picked up from home!"

Molly, meanwhile, had fished her paperback out of the cut, but it wasn't looking very readable. She shouted over to Milo again. "Tell her this book's ruined and she's going to pay for it!"

Milo was about to open his mouth, but the Captain stopped him. "No need! I think Danny's got the message."

Lorraine was confused. "Well, I certainly haven't."

"I think there's a dispute on of some kind!" the Captain explained.

Kevin felt he had to justify himself. "Yeah! The Boat Gang's falling apart, 'cos these lot are always complaining!"

Lorraine suspected Milo was included in "these lot" and rushed to defend the family honour. "Not our son, I'm sure – we're always very positive, us Marlows."

Milo felt wonderful to have his mum on his side for once. "Yeah. It's 'cos you lot are always bossing!"

Lorraine was about to say more, but the Captain put a hand on her arm. "I don't think it's family business – this, Lorraine. I think it's Boat Gang business."

Molly, still furious and getting more furious as she tried to lay the book out to dry in the sun, shouted over again. "Tell her it's one pound eighty pence, and there's a bookmark missin' an' all!"

But before there was any more shouting or family feuding the Captain stood up and spoke very clearly. "It definitely sounds like Boat Gang business – and I think it'd be a good idea for everyone if the Boat Gang had a meeting and sorted its business out!"

Chapter Ten

All of the Boat Gang members had been summoned, but nobody was quite sure what it was all about apart from Shebaz.

"It's about who's leader!"

"We haven't got a leader," said Ian.

"So why're Kevin and Danny always orderin' everybody about all the time!" asked Milo.

That started Brian off. "I'm on Kevin's side! 'Cos you order me around more than he does!"

"That's different. I'm your brother!"

Kevin had his own theory. "A gang's got to have a leader or we'd just argue all the time!"

"What do you think we're doing now?" asked Milo.

Liz and Suzi were sitting listening to all this from up on top of the boat.

"I hate arguments, don't you?" said Liz tetchily.

"No. I like a good shoutin' match!" said Suzi.

"No you don't! You're just saying that!"

"I do!"

Meanwhile, on the "floor of the house", Kevin was laying the blame. "Molly started all this."

"She just wanted to read her book," argued Milo.

"Where is she?" asked Shebaz, "an' where's Danny?"

Kevin answered him in a voice heavy with implication. "They're sortin' out their room!"

Up in the attic Molly was dragging her bed across the floor, while Danny was measuring the walls with a dressmaker's tape and chalking a line down what she had calculated was the middle of the room. "I've measured it exactly. You've got 3.79 metres, and I've got 3.95 to allow for the squiggly bit by the fireplace."

On Molly's "side" of the attic their mascot, "Babs the Bun", was propped up like a judge in sessions against her trunk. Molly ignored Danny, but spoke to the rabbit.

"Excuse me, Barbara Bunnyrabbit, but would you mind telling my fusspot sister that I couldn't care less about the squiggly bits and she can shove her head up the fireplace for all I care!"

Danny retaliated in kind. "An' you can tell my sister that I'm taking back the jeans I lent her," and then she darted across the line and liberated her stone-washed baggies.

It was war. "An' you can tell my sister that I'm taking back my trainers!" said Molly to the long-suffering toy rabbit. Danny whisked them off her feet and threw them at her.

"An' you can tell my sister Molly Maungeyface that she's to stay on her side and she's never to cross this line ever again."

"And you can tell my sister Danny Dogsbreath that I never want to go into her smelly half of the room anyway!"

The family business having been settled, Danny was anxious to sort the Gang business. "Right – I'm going over to the Boat Club!"

Danny dashed down the stairs. Molly, not wanting

Danny to tell tales about her behind her back, was about to run after her when she realised that this was impossible without "crossing the line"!

Molly paused at the border for a moment, gave a scream of rage and then deliberately invaded enemy territory.

By the time Danny and Molly arrived at the Boat Club there was a clear split between Ian, Tessa and Brian, who agreed with Kevin and Danny, versus Suzi, Liz and Shebaz, who were with Milo and Molly.

Each group was huddled around a different end of the workshop like American football teams discussing tactics. Now and then snatches of heated conversation could be heard above the discontented mumbling.

"There's more of us than there are of them!"

"No there isn't!"

"It doesn't matter anyway. We're the original Boat Gang!"

"I was in it before she was!"

"It's up to them. If they don't want to be in it they can clear off!"

"You tell 'em!"

And then, at exactly the same time, Kevin and Milo broke free from their groups and walked towards no man's land just under the prow of the boat.

Kevin spoke first. "It's up to you."

"No," said Milo. "It's up to you!"

Kevin considered this for a moment. "*What's* up to us?"

Milo looked behind to check his supporters were

there and folded his arms across his chest. "It's up to you lot if you want to stay in the gang or not."

"Oh no!" said Kevin, feeling the ground shift from under him. "That's up to *you lot*. If you don't like it, you don't have to be in it!"

Molly stepped forward to stand beside Milo. "We like it fine. You just wanna take it over. *You're* the rebels!"

Kevin retaliated. "*You're* the traitors. We're the proper Boat Gang. This is *our* headquarters – and that's *our* boat!!"

As Kevin pointed to the old boat, the boat that gave the Boat Gang its name, an idea came into Milo's head. "Go for it!"

Kevin knew exactly what they were going for. "Stop 'em!"

What followed resembled a scene from a swash-buckling pirate movie as both sides raced for the boat and tried to clamber on to it. There was uproar everywhere, with everyone running around and shouting and giving each other orders at once. Shebaz, with the advantage of being tall and still fit from his basketball training, managed to haul himself over the port side of the boat, hollering for support in real pirate fashion. "Follow me! This way, me hearties!"

But his boldness wilted as Tessa grabbed hold of his feet from below.

"Gerroff! Gerroff me! No! No tickling!"

Over on the starboard side, Molly was doing well and had pulled herself up and over the gunwales when she met with Danny and a bucket of sawdust and woodshavings.

"There you are!" cried Danny as she emptied the bucket over her sister's head. "Wash *that* out with Head and Shoulders!"

Milo had managed to find a rope hanging from a rail and had started climbing, but Kevin got the other end of it. For a few moments it was touch and go whether Milo would get to the top before Kevin could untie the knot, but Kevin had quick and nimble fingers, and Milo and the rope ended in a tangle on the floor.

In the midst of all this muddle and confusion Suzi and Liz crept aboard without the enemy spotting them. They appeared underneath the cabin and raised a cheer from their supporters until Tessa and Ian climbed onto the top of the cabin and dropped a large fishing net over their heads.

It looked like it was over. Milo, Shebaz and Molly launched one more attack, but Brian had found a water pistol from somewhere and was keeping them at bay with it, laughing to himself like a bad impersonation of Long John Silver in a Fish Finger advert.

Milo quickly retreated to a dry corner. Molly and Shebaz ran outside, and Suzi and Liz were still struggling in the net.

Kevin climbed onto the cabin of the boat and proclaimed victory. "Our Boat! Our Club! Our Gang!"

Danny joined him. "Be in it or buzz off!"

"Looks like Molly has already!" boasted Kevin.

"Gone back to finish her book!" suggested Danny scornfully.

"Oi, Captain Clever! Tell my megamouth sister that's where she's wrong!"

Kevin looked towards the door and saw that Molly hadn't gone for her book. She'd gone for a bucket of something sticky and wet that seemed to be mostly mud. Molly took a ladle full and raised it behind her head. Kevin could see what was coming – "Look out! Duck!" – but they had no time to get down from the top of the cabin before the first glob of mostly-mud struck Kevin squarely in the mush, while the next few shots fired in quick succession with deadly accuracy besplattered the others.

Molly was delighted with her success. "Bullseye! Gerrem, Shebaz!"

That was the signal for Shebaz, who had also been busy outside, to charge in with some old feather pillows and scatter the contents over the already clagged-up opposition. The effect was similar to being tarred and feathered – a sort of sticky chicken look.

The sticky chickens were making a lot of noise and trying to escape Molly, who was still flinging glob everywhere, even managing to accidentally land some on Suzi, who was worried about possible allergic reactions.

"If I get a rash I'm gonna tell my mum on you!"

In the midst of all this mayhem Kevin's dad, who hadn't been able to work for the racket, arrived at the door and tried to call Molly to order.

"Molly!!!"

Molly, hearing her name called and thinking that they had slipped around to attack her from the rear, scooped up an extra large ladle full of her special gungey mostly-mud preparation – and let fly without looking.

* * *

117

There must have been a small proportion of grease in the bottom of the bucket that Molly had mixed her mixture in, because the more they tried to rub it off the more they seemed to rub it in.

They didn't smell so good either.

Chris, still wiping his face, sat with Lynda on a bench strategically placed between the two rival factions, and gave them the hard word. "Number one–"

Kevin let out a plaintive "daaaaad!", but Lynda gave him the even harder word. "Number one: don't interrupt!"

Chris continued. "Number two: what you delinquents use as Gang Headquarters is part of my workshop."

Kevin tried again. "But daaaad!"

Lynda stopped him dead. "Number three: no whining! Number four –"

Chris took over again. "Number four: I don't want my workshop used as a battleground for Bugsy Malone-type warfare!"

Kevin persisted against the odds. "Yes but –" and then Lynda put the kibosh on the lot. "Number five: no excuses! Number six: the Boat Club's locked up, and it's stayin' locked till the fightin' and feudin' is over and done with!"

Later that evening, when the dust had settled and most of the muck had been scraped off, each of the four main protagonists sought out someone to speak their mind to.

Kevin sat in conference with the Captain on her boat. "Our name's been dragged in the mud!"

"And who's to blame for that?"

"The kids who gunged up me dad – *and I wasn't one of them*!"

Milo slumped in an armchair and moaned to his mum. "I can take a joke, you know. I just don't like bein' taken for granted."

"I've always been the same myself."

"It's Kevin's fault – an' now we *all* look stupid!"

Molly holed-up in the attic and gave Chris an earful. "When she says jump, I gotta jump – she thinks I'm her pet flea! All I wanted was a bit of peace!"

"Well you've got peace now, haven't you?"

"No – I've got *non-stop war*!"

Danny dried the dishes for Lynda and opened her heart. "I just want everyone to have a good time, an' not mope about all day!"

"You can try too hard."

"You have to – 'cos there's some people make *no effort at all*!"

The four adults listened and then made their suggestions.

"Maybe you should meet 'em half-way," the Captain suggested to Kevin.

"Talk it over nicely," said Lorraine to her son.

"Make peace!" Chris told Molly.

"Why not compromise?" Lynda asked Danny.

And then, as if by telepathical synchronological magic, at exactly the same moment, in four different places, Kevin, Milo, Danny and Molly came out with exactly the same phrase:

"NO WAY!"

Chapter Eleven

The continuing internal disputes of the Boat Gang were provoking regular summit conferences of interested adults in the Pollys' kitchen.

"They're rebuilding the Berlin Wall in our attic, you know!" complained Lynda.

Lorraine had evidently seen it all coming. "I knew those two girls were going to cause trouble."

Lynda didn't agree at all. "Rubbish! Your lads are just as much to blame as anybody!"

Chris took a philosophical view. "It always gets like this at the end of the summer holidays. They'll simmer down soon."

The Captain saw storm clouds ahead. "I don't think they're simmering, Mister Polly! I think they're just coming to the boil."

Of all these different opinions the Captain's was closest to the truth. Even as they discussed and worried in the kitchen, elsewhere the final show-down was taking place.

Over at the canal bridge it looked like a rehearsal for *West Side Story*.

Molly, Milo, Shebaz, Suzi and Liz were marching over from the fields to the towpath. Danny, Kevin, Brian, Tessa and Ian were coming the other way.

Two feet from the middle of the bridge both parties came to a silent stop and glared at each other. Neither side was ready to give way, and it looked like going the way of all "Jets" and "Sharks" and ending in tragedy.

The sun shone down. The suspense music started in their heads. They knew they couldn't turn round and they knew that as soon as someone made a move to push past there was going to be a scrap.

And then –

"Hiya!"

– a voice from below, and it wasn't the Guardian of the Bridge. It was a young boy about the same age as the rest of them, wearing reactolite shades and dressed in a casual continental style with light denim slacks and a trendy silk blouson over a black T-shirt.

He'd changed his image, but not so much that Kevin couldn't recognise him. "Hiya!"

Milo recognised him too. "Hiya, Joe! When did you get back?"

Kevin's and Milo's eyes lit up together, not entirely because they were pleased to see Joe Mackavoy, but because, not for the first time, they had both had the same idea at the same time.

The summit conference of the big four was still ongoing in the kitchen when Molly, Kevin, Danny and Milo crashed through the door in a state of high excitement.

Chris felt he ought to pass on the mood of the meeting – "Look, Kevin, we're all rather worried – " but was interrupted by Kevin – "There's no need – " who was interrupted in his turn by Chris – "There's every need! We don't want gang warfare!"

Kevin sat down to explain. "It's OK, dad! There won't be any more fighting."

"Good," said Chris, feeling the wind spill from his sails.

"That's nice," said Lorraine breezily. "You've all made friends again."

"No," said Molly.

Lorraine wished she'd not spoken.

"No," said Danny. "We've decided that the gang with the most members is the proper Boat Gang –"

"– And the rest of them have left it," explained Kevin.

"Only we don't know which is which yet," added Milo.

"Neither do we," said Lynda, all hope of a peace settlement banished, "and until we do, Boat Gang Headquarters is staying under lock and key!"

Kevin was still cheerily optimistic. "It'll all be sorted by tomorrow."

Milo agreed. "Yeah – soon as Joe makes up his mind!"

Joe was enjoying making up his mind. He sat in Kevin's room, in Kevin's swivel computer chair, eating the chips that Kevin had just bought him, while Kevin, Danny, and Brian gave him their full concentration.

"Thanks for the chips. Not bad for English ones."

"Joe's been abroad with his dad," explained Kevin for Danny's benefit.

"Joe leaned back and swivelled a little. "I had a great time," and then, examining the chip on the way to his mouth, "You get good chips in France – frites, they call 'em. They eat 'em with salad cream in Belgium."

Brian didn't like the idea of chips and salad cream. "Eugh!" But Kevin wanted to keep Joe sweet till he'd made his mind up. "Shurrup, Brian!"

Danny offered Joe a can of pop in case he was thirsty after the chips. Joe accepted graciously, and continued with his continental anecdotes. "In Germany, you know, you can get your chips with sausages an' curry sauce."

"You get that here!" said Danny, but Joe sighed at her ignorance and put her right.

"It's different over there. The sausages are more squodgey." Then he burped, put down his can, and went back to his original theme. "Spanish chips are different again – more like little roast potatoes!"

Kevin tried to look as impressed as he could manage. "Great."

Joe stood up, walked over to Kevin's bed and stretched out on it. It was very continental to have a rest after a meal.

"What's been goin' on in the gang then?" he inquired as he lay back. "I thought there'd be nobody left."

"There wasn't for a bit," said Kevin truthfully.

Joe looked over at Danny in a worried sort of way. "I dunno why you let girls in!"

Danny shot to attention – ready for action. "You what?!"

Kevin intervened swiftly before all his hard work was lost. "Danny's me cousin. We had to, really."

Danny narrowed her eyes. She didn't like the sound of all this, but there was a good reason for holding her tongue just now.

Kevin continued. "The thing is, Joe – are you on our side or theirs?"

Joe closed his eyes and breathed deeply. "I don't know."

Joe mustn't have had quite enough chips to settle his appetite because later that evening he was sitting in pride of place in the divided attic, on Molly's famous trunk, with Molly, Milo and Shebaz feeding him double-decker sandwiches.

Joe was continuing with his continental revelations. "French bread's great, you know! It's dead crispy an' whiter than ours. Mind you, it goes like rock when it's stale."

Molly noticed that he'd stopped chewing. "You want another sandwich?"

"Thanks. German bread's a bit chewy, an' it's got a lot of bits in – an' you get it with cheese an' meat for breakfast."

Shebaz looked pale at the thought of cheese for breakfast but Joe ignored him.

"Spanish breakfast is best – tostada! It's like toast only done in the frying pan, and you can have it with jam."

There was a pause in the conversation, mainly because Joe had his mouth full. He seemed to be munching away happily on his sandwiches – even though they were English and he'd already had a bag of chips.

Milo thought it was time to put the question. "Are you gonna be on our side or theirs?"

Joe swallowed and considered this question while he picked a gritty bit of granary bread out of his teeth. "Well, they said I could be third in command – after Kevin an' Danny – but I dunno about girls bein' in charge."

Molly's eyes glared like beacons. "What!"

Milo winced. "We don't exactly have anyone in charge," he said shamelessly, "– at the moment."

Next morning, at ten o'clock, Joe was sitting at one of the outside café tables with the Kevin-Danny faction. Kevin had reached a heart-breaking but politically necessary decision. "Yeah, OK, Joe – you can borrow my computer if you want."

"Thanks, Kev."

Danny was shocked at this bolt from the blue. "What?"

But there was worse to come. Joe leaned over the table and spoke in the gravelled tones of a mafia boss. "An' I'm the new gang leader – right?"

Before Kevin could sell his soul and sign in blood the Molly-Milo faction arrived on the scene and interrupted proceedings.

Milo had urgent business with Joe. "Hold on – we wanna have a word!"

Shebaz made the offer. "Look Joe, we don't have any leaders, but you can be our chairperson. It's the same thing really."

Joe adjusted his reactolites and considered it carefully.

Kevin moved closer and hissed in his ear. "You said you were on our side. We're the Boat Gang! They're the traitors!"

Molly heard this and went for Kevin with murder in her eyes. "*You're* the traitors, Kevin Polly!"

Joe pushed his chair away from the table and stood up. He was going to speak. He was going to decide.

He waited till there was silence.

"The way I see it – you lot want me to be leader," – nodding at Kevin and Danny's mob – "and you lot want me to be chairperson," – indicating the Molly and Milo crew. "So why don't I be leader *and* chairperson, and you can all be in my gang."

They were gobsmacked, all of them, but it was logical.

"Why not?" asked Joe. "No more trouble."

"Well –" said Kevin, unsure exactly how they'd arrived at this point.

"Well –" said Milo, equally unsure.

Joe continued, taking their approval for granted. "I dunno about girls though."

Danny wasn't quite as dazed as the rest. "You what?"

Neither was Molly. "Yeah? What is it you don't know about girls, Joe?"

Joe explained. "Well, I want it to be a top gang now I'm in charge."

"And?" asked Molly and Danny together.

Joe had been away since Kevin's cousins had arrived to stay. Joe didn't know how thin the ice was that he was walking on. "An' girls aren't really as tough as boys, are they?" he said confidently.

Lynda and Chris were in the bedroom folding sheets when they heard the screams.

"I think the Captain was right," said Lynda, worried. "I think it's come to the boil."

Another scream followed, louder and more urgent than the first.

"Sounds like it's boiling over!" said Chris, as they dropped the sheet they were holding between them and ran downstairs.

* * *

When they arrived in the garden Chris and Lynda had no trouble discovering the source of the screaming.

Joe Mackavoy was being carried down the towpath towards the bridge, with Tessa leading the way and one of the other girls on each arm and leg. He was struggling a lot and screaming a lot, but it wasn't doing any good.

"Help! Gerremoffme! Help! Fellers! Help me!"

But the "fellers" were neither willing nor able to help. They were doubled up, helpless with laughter.

"Where are they taking him?" asked Chris.

"Over the back fields," said Kevin in between attacks of the giggles. "They're gonna roll him down the hill!"

Brian remembered an experience he'd had recently. "He'd better watch out for the nettles!"

Even as they contemplated this, the sound of an even more piercing scream was carried towards them on the summer's breeze.

Next day all the gang minus Joe gathered together in the Boat Club.

Tessa looked about for him in vain. "I can't see our new Leader and Chairperson anywhere!"

Danny laughed. "I think he's gone off on his travels again."

"Maybe he's gone to find out what else he doesn't know about girls," suggested Tessa. "Are you and Molly friends now?"

Danny grinned at Molly. "'Course we are. We're always falling out, us!"

Molly put her arm round Danny. "We're dead close, really!"

This was great news. Ian and Shebaz were delighted.

"So we're all mates again – and everything's back to normal!"

For a few seconds it was. For a few seconds! Then the hopeful silence was broken by two familiar voices.

"Oh yeah?" said one voice.

"Who says?" said the other.

Nobody had noticed Kevin and Milo, sitting as far away from each other as possible, on opposite sides of the room, glaring at each other with undiminished hostility.

Chapter Twelve

It had been the wettest summer since Oliver Cromwell, and he'd seen some of the wettest summers since the Precambrian era. But Kevin and his cousins were now living in the Prescholastic era – the time before the end of the summer holidays when the sun blazes down on schoolkids everywhere to warm them up for the new term.

Last month the reservoirs had been overflowing. This month the water authorities had declared a drought, and Brian Marlow was doing his bit to help by quenching his thirst exclusively with pop and ice cream.

Liz and Suzi had been waiting outside the Mynstone Stores for him to come out with theirs, and had read the poster in the window two million times before he appeared with three cornets – two single-dollop economy cones and a three-cornered chocolate, strawberry and vanilla with nuts on for himself.

Suzi was jealous but concerned. "You'll make yourself ill, you will."

"I burn it off," explained Brian. "What's this?"

Liz was looking at the poster for the two million and oneth time in case she'd missed anything. "It's about the Carnival Procession," she said.

Brian licked his ice cream and flicked back his hair with pride. "Our float won a silver medal last year. It was called 'Space Battle Heroes From Delta Three'! We built a cardboard rocket on Joe's dad's lorry."

Liz and Suzi didn't look as impressed as Brian thought they should. "It was Kev's idea," he added.

Suzi wasn't interested in the past. "What about this year, then? It's on Saturday week!"

Brian wasn't optimistic. "Kev's had no time to think of anythin'. He's too busy with me brother."

"What doin'?" asked Liz.

Brian bit the end off his cornet and told her straight. "Arguing."

Kevin, Milo, Danny and Molly were sitting in the attic in absolute stillness. The morning sun beamed through the windows and lit the particles of dust that danced in the air above their heads. Babs the Bun sat next to them, wearing Danny's Pulsatrone Sports Power Alarm with stopwatch feature and lap counter.

Kevin opened his eyes, looked shocked for a second as he realised where he was, and then broke the silence. "Go on then!"

Milo raised his head from his rack of letters, most of which were Es. "It's you!"

Kevin raised his voice a pitch. "It's *you*!"

Milo matched his pitch and raised him another pitch. "No. IT'S YOU!"

"Beepeepeepeepeepeepeepeeeeep," Babs the Bun pitched in with Danny's pre-set Power Alarm, and Danny came to life. "Sorry, Kev! Too late! Babs the Bun says 'time's up'."

Kevin flew at Milo. "You lost me a turn – you dozy maggot! I spent so long waiting for you I fell asleep!"

Milo defended himself. "It's not my fault if you're a sloth-brain, Kevin Polly!"

Molly yawned. "Give it a rest, you two. Me an' Danny have had enough."

Danny picked up Babs and did a silly squeaky rabbit voice for her. "Babs the Bun says 'You're no fun!'"

Kevin and Milo didn't laugh. They hadn't laughed for a week. Molly thought it was time to make a speech she'd been composing while they'd been playing Scrabble. "Look – we thought we were gonna have a bad time, stayin' here for the summer." She turned to look at Kevin. "You were a bit –"

Danny interrupted. "You were a pig to us!"

"I wasn't!"

"You were!"

Molly continued. "– But it's great now, 'cos we're all together – boys an' girls in the same gang. The only thing is –"

Danny put her oar in again. "The thing is – are you two gonna make friends, or do we have to roll you down the hill like we did Joe Mackavoy?"

Kevin looked sulkily at Milo. "It's him."

Milo looked sulkily back. "It's not me. It's him!"

"He's supposed to be me mate," Kevin complained, "an' all he does now is wind me up all the time."

"You mean, I argue back."

"Look Milo –"

"Dennis! Dennis is me name! Dennis Marlow!"

This was quite a shock to Molly and Danny, who'd never heard him called anything but Milo and thought it was his first name. Kevin was scathing about this innovation. "You've always been Milo!"

But Milo was on the attack now. "Oh yeah – and do you know what they used to call him in the Infants? Polly Parrot! Little Polly Parrotface!"

Kevin retaliated. "Yeah, well listen 'Milky Milo' – if I hadn't stuck up for you at school you'd be squashed flat by now! 'Cos you're a worm!"

That was enough for Milo, who threw his Scrabble letters at Kevin, and stamped out of the room.

Molly called after him "Milo!" and then, too late, "Denn-is!"

Kevin picked up the scattered Es, and shook his head. "He can't take a joke these days."

"Who's joking?" asked Danny. "We've only got a little bit of holiday left and we don't want you spoilin' it – Parrotface!"

And then the two girls ran down the stairs after Milo, leaving Kevin speechless – and wordless as well.

Brian had finished his ice cream and was sitting with Joe Mackavoy in the Polly Garden Café when Milo walked past them in a thunderous huff.

"Whassup Milo?" Brian called after him.

Milo didn't even stop. "Dennis!! I'm your brother and I'm called Dennis!" he snapped, and walked off home under the only cloud in the sky.

Joe lay back with his feet on the table in a lazy insolent way and shrugged philosophically.

"C'est la vie, monsieur! – That's what the French say."

Brian had trouble with English, let alone French. "What's that mean?"

"It's just a sayin'," explained Joe, who had no

132

idea what it meant. "– an' then they bring you halfa loafa crispy bread with loadsa cheese in it!"

Brian liked the sound of that. "Wow!"

Joe picked up his wholemeal scone and bit into it without much relish. "'Fromage sandwich' – that's what they call it. Better than this rubbish!"

As he bit into it, Molly and Danny, no particular friends of his to put it mildly, advanced on him from the doorway. He didn't see them until it was too late.

"Excusez-moi, monsieur," said Molly, firmly and politely. "Do you mind gettin' your smelly feet off our Aunty Lynda's table!"

He didn't, so Danny made sure he understood. "Right now! Or we'll bounce you down the towpath."

Joe dropped his legs and stood up. "I wanna see Kevin."

Molly blocked his way. "What about?"

Joe wasn't in the mood for losing any more face in front of Brian. "It's private," he declared. "Scusez-moi!"

Not wishing to have a rumpus with customers about, Molly and Danny stepped out of the way to let him through. Joe saw this as a victory and turned to give a cocky grin to Brian as he sauntered past.

This was too much provocation for Danny, who couldn't resist leaving her foot out so that Joe stumbled over it. As he went flying, Danny put on an expression of deep continental concern. "Oh pardon, monsieur! Scusez-moi!"

"Don't think I'm scared of 'em, 'cos I'm not!" Having made it to the safety of Kevin's room, Joe

133

felt free to put the record straight. "They get away with it 'cos they're girls!"

"Yeah," Kevin agreed automatically.

"An' they never rolled me down the hill – I just went along with it for a laugh."

Kevin didn't argue. "'course!"

And then Joe got to 'le crunch'. "Anyway, you can't have me dad's truck for the float this year – 'cos I'm not in the gang any more!"

The silver medal from last year was still on display on the sideboard downstairs. Kevin didn't hesitate. "OK – you're in the gang! All right!"

Joe's reply came as a shock. "I don't wanna be in it."

"Why not?"

Joe gave his very personal views an airing. "It's no good any more. You don't *do* anything!"

Kevin started to tell him some of the things they'd done while Joe was away, but he dismissed them with a sneer.

"That's all sissy stuff. You were gonna get the boat fixed, an' play American football. We used to do really dangerous stuff, like when I dared Nick Robinson to climb over that sewer pipe. You've gone soft. The whole gang's gone soft 'cos it's been taken over by girls!"

Kevin flushed, and gave an embarrassed "Get lost!" It was just as he had feared in his worst nightmares. Is this what the boys at school would be saying about him? Joe continued –

"An' your mate Milo's the worst 'cos he follers them about like a big drip!"

"That's rubbish!" said Kevin, but it all made sense. That's what had happened to Milo. That's why they weren't mates any more.

Joe saw his advantage. "Yeah? Well, me an' the boys down our street are gonna do our own float for the Carnival on me dad's truck – an' we're gonna win!"

"No chance!" cried Kevin, suddenly finding his fighting spirit.

Joe walked to the door. "Well, it'll beat anythin' your girly gang'll do! If you wanna win a gold medal this year – come an' join us!"

For some time after Joe had left Kevin sat on his bed thinking. Joe had unsettled him but hadn't quite knocked him off his perch. He knew well enough that Joe was all mouth, and despite all the arguing Kevin still felt patriotic about the Boat Gang. He still felt it was *his* gang, and he was going to make sure the Boat Gang of Mynstone Locks won another medal to go on *his* sideboard.

Brian was late for the emergency meeting in the Boat Club that afternoon, but nobody had noticed. They were all busy examining sheets of paper from Kevin's tech drawing book.

"It's Kev's idea for a float for the Carnival," Liz explained to him.

"It's the same as last year," Shebaz whispered, but Kevin heard him.

"It's completely different! Last year it was a space ship!"

"And this year," said Tessa, with just a trace of sarcasm, "it's an Atomstar Battlestation Earth-defence War-satellite!"

Brian approved. "Brilliant!" and started bouncing about in his *ballet dancer with fleas* mode, making imagined outer space battle noises.

"Eouuuuu! Kakakakakaka! Shtum shtum shtum!"

Milo became aware that his younger brother had arrived. "Who let you in?"

"Shurrup, Milky Milo!" answered Brian, in a cheekier way than he would normally have addressed his brother had he not spent so much time with Joe recently.

Milo tried to grab Brian, but he dodged out of the way behind Kevin, who Milo noted had a smile on his face.

"Where do we get a truck then?" asked Danny. "Is that what Joe came about?"

Kevin coughed and addressed the meeting. "We're not using Joe's truck," he said, as though it was all his own decision. "We're using dad's van done up as a Space Station. Some of us sit on the roof, an' the others walk behind."

"What as?" asked Molly.

"As the Battlestation Crew. We can use the boiler suits and helmets from last year."

"It's all just like last year!" Milo complained.

Kevin had been waiting for Milo to start trouble. "You think of something better, then! I'm fed up being the one who comes up with all the ideas!"

Milo looked away. Nobody dared speak in case they were expected to have an idea. Then a most unlikely voice was raised on another unlikely person's behalf.

"Liz has got an idea," said Suzi.

"Shush!" said Liz who didn't want any attention.

"She has!"

"I haven't!"

"She's sitting on it!" said Suzi, and pulling a

sketchpad out from under Liz passed it to Tessa. Tessa turned the cover over and was instantly engrossed. "Hey! It's good, this!"

Soon everybody was crowding round to have a look. It was a real work of art – all sorts of costumes and a design for the float as well. The theme was giant insects and other garden creatures – caterpillars, spiders, wasps, ladybirds, aphids, even slugs – a sort of magnified micro-world of garden monsters.

"It's a Micro-wildlife Float," said Tessa.

"Yeah," said Ian. "Save the Worm!"

Suzi thought it was a great idea as long as she wasn't the one who had to be the worm.

It seemed like "Atomstar Battlestation" was out and "Micro-wildlife" was in. Kevin wasn't going to let it happen – a weedy idea like that wasn't going to win any medals.

"Dressin' up as insects – it's pathetic!"

Liz looked hurt at this outburst. She was ready to sit on her design again, but Milo came quickly to her defence. "Ignore him, Liz. He's only jealous!"

Kevin was outraged. "You what!" he spluttered.

Milo didn't back down. "Just 'cos you didn't think of it!"

"Get lost, Milo!"

It looked like another squabble between Kevin and Milo but Danny came in on Milo's side. "I think Milo's right!"

And Molly backed her up. "Yeah, me too!"

Kevin glanced round the rest of the gang and could see from the expressions on their faces that he was on to a loser. He'd done his best for them and this was how they treated him. A red mist formed in front of his eyes and his mouth went into gear without any consultation with his brain. "I'll tell you who's right – *Joe's* right! This was a great gang – an' now it's been taken over by girls it's gone soft! Well you can do what you like now! I'm packin' it in!"

It was quite a powerful dramatic moment when Kevin strode out of the Boat Gang Headquarters for ever and ever, and it would have been even more powerful if Brian hadn't have jumped up and decided to join him.

"And me! I'm packin' it in an' all!"

Kevin sighed to himself as he walked away. It was clear he didn't relish the thought of a life of exile with Brian as his inseparable companion.

Chapter Thirteen

Kevin's dad was trying to do the washing up. Lynda was trying to do the accounts for the carpentry business. Between them was Lorraine, with her coffee in one hand, a biscuit in the other, and her mouth open.

The day of the Carnival Procession was fast approaching, and Lorraine had taken to wearing an enormous pink paper rosette in her lapel with the word "COMMITTEE" inscribed in the centre.

Danny and Molly had asked her a fairly innocent question about it, and now she was making sure that everyone listened to her while she answered it – at length.

"All floats have to have an entry number. If it's *in* the procession it *has* to be registered. It's all in the book."

Lorraine indicated a large folder on the table. Molly picked it up and read the label. "Carnival Procession Committee Rules."

Lorraine shook her head. "There's no need to read it all. I can tell you now – if it's not registered it's not eligible, and if it's not eligible it can't win a prize."

"Can we register then, please?" asked Molly.

Lorraine placed her biscuit and coffee on the table, wiped her hands, sat down and opened the file. "Late registrations," she announced, "have to put it to the Committee." Then, plucking a biro from her pocket and clicking it in readiness, "Do you have a vehicle?"

They weren't sure. Danny went over to the sink to talk to Chris. "Can we use the van, Uncle Chris?"

Chris was puzzled. "Kev's already asked me that, an' then he came back again later an' said you didn't need it any more!"

Lorraine tutted with displeasure at all this incompetence and slammed shut her folder. Danny and Molly headed for the stairs with one thought between them.

"What's he playing at?"

The red felt-penned sign on the outside of Kevin's door had reappeared again – this time in even heavier lettering. "PRIVATE – KEEP OUT – THIS MEANS YOU!"

Danny and Molly ignored it and tapped on the door.

"Who's that?" said Kevin from inside.

"It's us," called Molly.

"Go away!"

"We just want to talk."

Footsteps – and then the door opened fractionally. But it was Joe's face that appeared at the gap. "He says 'Go away!'"

And then Brian's face appeared below Joe's. "And that means 'Go away!'"

To help make his point Brian produced his water pistol and started squirting at them, brave in the knowledge that he could duck back inside Kevin's room. What he didn't expect to happen was that Joe would grab him by the scruff of the neck, and thrust him through the door, slamming it behind him. "Here y'are! Take him with you!"

Facing the wet and angry faces of Molly and Danny, Brian gulped with fear, dropped the pistol and put his hands in the air. "Peace!"

It didn't look like he was going to get any!

Behind the door Joe and Kevin were laughing at their joke and admiring their own cleverness.

"See!" said Joe, "they came crawling straight away. Bound to, weren't they!"

"Yeah," said Kevin. "Why?"

Joe despaired of him. "'Cos they know their idea's naff an' they're after yours, of course!"

Kevin was flattered. "Do y'think so?"

Joe encouraged him. "It's obvious!"

Kevin picked up his plan and rolled it up purposefully. "Yeah, well they're too late."

"What's it called, again?" asked Joe, trying to disguise the fact that he had completely forgotten.

"Atomstar Battlestation Earthdefence War-satellite!" answered Kevin without having to look.

Joe clapped him on the back. "It's a winner!"

Kevin knew it was. "It'll beat their stupid insect thing!"

Joe smirked with confidence. "They won't even get theirs done in time!"

Whatever Joe thought about their chances of getting the Micro-wildlife Float ready, it was clear that no one in the Boat Gang believed him. The Boat Club was a busy hive of insect-making activity.

Liz and Suzi staggered in with piles of old newspapers. Ian and Tessa arrived with rolls of wire and fabric. Shebaz, looking like Superman, carried in some enormous blocks of polystyrene. Milo came with a barrowload of junk from his house – mostly egg cartons. Danny brought the paints and brushes and glue, borrowed from Uncle Chris, and Molly came with a very important sack of flour.

In no time at all Ian and Tessa were cutting fabric and twisting the wire into shapes, Shebaz was hacking away at the polystyrene and getting little white bobbles everywhere, and Molly was getting buckets of water for the flour "paste".

Danny and Milo stood with Liz, looking at her original sketches, like two building site foremen with the architect.

"It's not gonna be exactly like your drawing, Liz," warned Danny. "We haven't got the time."

"It's rubbish that, anyway," said Liz.

"She's a genius!" said Suzi, enthusiastically.

"I did it in ten minutes."

That confirmed it for Suzi. "That's what all geniuses say!"

In another corner Shebaz was making a model of a wasp's nest out of the polystyrene, but in the process he'd given himself a bad attack of white bobbly dandruff.

Milo stood watching him work and worried aloud. "Kevin's would have been dead easy to do."

Shebaz shook his head, creating a polystyrene snowstorm. "An' dead boring! It was the same costumes as last year."

Danny had an inspiration. "They were boiler suits, weren't they?"

"Yeah – they're in a box somewhere."

142

"We can use them as a base, an' stick things on to make costumes. It'll save a load of time!"

Liz and Sue had found themselves the demanding job of tearing up paper to make papier mâché. Liz was having second thoughts about her reputation. "I don't wanna be a genius, Suze – it's dead embarrassin'."

Suzi reassured her. "You're not a genius at everythin', Liz."

"No?" asked Liz innocently.

"No," said Suzi, with a completely straight face. "Mostly you're thick as a brick."

Liz looked her back straight in the eyes with the same expression. "That's all right then, Suzi."

Next minute there was paper flying everywhere, but somewhere in the middle of it they were either laughing or making a noise very much like it.

It was looking as though Joe had been very wrong. They were going to make it in time.

Danny had found the old boiler suits in the boat and had dressed Milo in one, with some prototype antennae on his head and one of Tessa's wire shell-like frames ready for his back.

"It's a cutaneous shell," said Tessa knowledgeably. "It's what ladybirds have on their backs!"

"You look dead cute," said Molly. Milo winced.

"Don't upset him," warned Tessa, "or he'll go off an' join Kev's Battlestation Crew!"

Milo didn't think so. "You're jokin' – I'd rather be a cutaneous ladybird than be on the same float as that skunk!"

The skunk in question was sweating under a hot sun trying to sift through a pile of metal scrap in Joe's dad's yard. Kevin was hot and tired, and slightly more hot and tired than Joe, who had been doing more organising than lifting, but was equally proud of their achievement.

"It's good stuff, innit?"

"It's heavy!"

"It'll make a great Battle Station!"

Kevin had heard enough talk from Joe about things that hadn't happened, and time was running out. "When are we gonna fix it on the truck then?"

Joe hesitated. "When me dad's not using it – the day before the Carnival."

"And where's all these mates of yours that are supposed to be helping us?"

"They'll be here!" insisted Joe, as though Kevin had no cause to pester him about such trivialities. "Manyana, man – don't get heavy."

But Kevin's faith was already shaken. "And what about costumes? We'll have no time!"

"That's your job," said Joe, pleased to pass the buck. "You said you'd got them already."

Kevin looked more worried. "Oh yeah – the boiler suits an' that."

"Yeah. Where are they?"

Kevin put his head in his hands. The worry was a big worry.

The sunshine that had frazzled Joe and Kevin had brought out a larger flock of gongoozlers than usual, and Lynda was rushed off her feet with orders. Naturally Lorraine had chosen that very time to arrive with her rosette and her folder of regulations to speak to Molly about the Carnival Procession. Lynda had asked her to go and discuss

144

it in the attic, but Lorraine had insisted that she was only popping in – something she had never done, and was incapable of doing.

"I'm pleased to tell you," she announced, "that the Committee have granted a provisional Late Registration Number '23' for a float called 'Micro-wildlife', entered by the Boat Gang at Mynstone Locks."

Molly was relieved. "We're in the Procession then?"

"Provisionally. But I must tell you that we're only allowed twenty-three floats by the local police and Joe Mackavoy and Kevin Polly also have a provisional late entry permit."

Molly was devastated. Lynda didn't understand. "Are you doing two floats?"

Molly started to explain. "No – well, yes. Well we're not – but you see Milo has fallen out with our Kevin and –"

She didn't get a chance to finish, or even properly start, because Danny came in, grabbed her by the arm and ran off with her. "Molly! Quick!"

Lorraine tutted again and shut her folder. "They were hiding something. I can tell, you know – it's a mother's instinct."

Lynda hoped there wouldn't be another all-out war. Lorraine didn't think so. "Not this time. This looks like the kind of disagreement you get between old friends. It never lasts long."

"Oh no?" asked Lynda in a voice loaded with meaning. Lorraine continued blithely. "I mean, there's plenty of things you do that irritate *me*."

"Such as?" asked Lynda, astonished.

Lorraine swigged her coffee and picked up her

folder. "Such as the way you always carry on working when I'm talking to you – but I never complain about it."

Over in the Boat Club everyone was silently busy. Liz and Suzi were stirring a binful of papier mâché paste. Ian, Tessa and Shebaz were painting up the costumes they'd already made – wings, shells, sets of six legs and antennae for ants, and a giant fabric and wire slug. Nobody spoke, and nobody stopped working, while up on the deck of the boat Milo and Kevin were having a stand-up Mutiny on the Bounty battle about the boiler suits.

Kevin had come to get them. "They're ours! The boiler suits go with my idea!"

"We're changing 'em!"

"You can't do that! You've got no right!"

"What are you afraid of? Do you think our 'pathetic idea' is gonna beat yours?"

While everyone's eyes were on this ding-dong argument they didn't notice Joe had sneaked through the door, and was about to settle the debate in a different way – until Danny came back through the door with Molly and caught him in the act.

"Look out! He's nickin' 'em!"

Everyone turned from Kevin and Milo and saw Joe standing there, large as life, with the bundle of overalls in his arms.

Joe went for the big bluff. "Yeah! What you gonna do about it!"

And then he saw the look on Tessa's face as she put down her paint pot, and decided on a different tactic.

146

Joe ran one way round the boat, followed by Tessa. Ian went the other way to head him off, but Joe managed to sidestep at the right moment and Tessa and Ian collided like express trains.

Joe was laughing, but Shebaz was coming for him, wielding a large block of polystyrene. It was light stuff but it looked dangerous enough. Joe threw the boiler suits to Kevin, and ducked out of the way. Kevin made a run for it but chose the wrong direction and walked straight into Molly and Danny.

Kevin gave up the struggle, but then he heard Joe's voice from the far corner by the door. "Let him go – or it's red and yeller gloss all over!"

Joe had a big pot of paint in each hand. It was another classic scene from a Ronald Reagan Western. Joe knew how the lines should go. "Right! Me and Kev are gonna walk out of here with those overalls and anyone trying to stop us is gonna get decorated!!!"

Everyone stopped in their tracks as though they'd seen the same movie – apart from Liz and Suzi, who must have seen a better one, and were moving slowly and imperceptibly along the top of the boat.

Joe was enjoying the upper hand. "Out of the way, you scumbags! We're comin' through!"

Joe and Kevin were just below the boat when Liz and Suzi reached their destination – the dustbin full of flour paste and soggy paper.

It took a while to get Joe cleaned up and into a borrowed shirt of Kevin's. His hair had set into a stiff clump of dried paste but it looked no worse

147

than if he'd been using a tube of some Superslick Salon-Exclusive Jelli-Conditioner (just glue it and go!).

The main protagonists had been called over to the house by Lorraine and Lynda – who were still just about talking to each other – to hear some dread-hot news.

Lynda laid it on the line. "Let's sort a few things out. There's no point in carrying on this argument because there's only going to be one float entered."

"It's a Committee decision," announced Lorraine, and then, taking two pieces of coloured paper out of her folder, she wrote a name on each, and put them into Chris's ancient relic of a flat hat.

Kevin and Milo were still making alternative suggestions. "We could race for it!" "We could arm wrestle for it!" But Lorraine wouldn't listen.

"The Committee have decided to draw a name out of a hat."

The arguments subsided. There was some consternation when Lorraine passed the hat to Brian but before anyone could object he'd dipped his hand in, pulled out one of the folded bits of paper, and given it to his mum.

Lorraine then took a thousand years to unfold it, adjust her specs, clear her throat and, when she was sure that everybody was climbing up the walls, declare, "Float number 23 in the procession will be the 'Atomstar Battlestation Earthdefence War-satellite'!"

The losers slumped in their chairs. Joe banged the table. "Yeah! We're official! Atomstar for gold!"

Chapter Fourteen

The sun continued to boil down on Joe's dad's yard, and Kevin continued to do most of the work on the float. They had started to bolt the scrap metal together to make the frame of the "Atomstar".

Brian had joined them but his main contribution was to lie on his back and lick ice lollies.

Joe was still crowing about their "triumph" in getting picked for the Carnival. "That showed 'em."

Kevin lifted his head from out of the Battle-station Centre of Operations, an old motorbike sidecar. He was unhappy about everything. "How did it show 'em?"

"We won."

"We didn't! We're entered, that's all. Now we'll never know if we're better than them or not."

"We know *that*."

"In *our* heads, yeah – but Milo doesn't know in *his* head!"

As far as Joe was concerned all this was techni-cal. "We got the boiler suits!"

Kevin couldn't seem to make Joe understand. "'Cos they don't need 'em any more. They've done all that work for nothing!"

This sounded like sympathy for the enemy to Joe. "Hey, Kev! Don't start gerrin' soft on 'em!"

Brian licked his lolly lazily and agreed. "Yeah! They deserve to lose for being so dim!"

There was something suspiciously self-satisfied in his tone.

"How's that?" asked Kevin.

Brian took another slurp on his four-stage rocket booster and explained. "Me mum wrote the names on different coloured paper."

Kevin came out from the sidecar. "What?!"

"Only slightly different – the bit with your name on it was more yellow. I was the only one who noticed! Smart, eh?"

Kevin was now standing over Brian, blocking out the sun.

Brian looked up at him and saw thunder clouds gathering. "What's wrong, Kev?"

Half an hour later, dragged into the Boat Club and surrounded by angry faces, Brian knew something wasn't right, but he was still defending his sneaky subterfuge. "I couldn't help looking, could I?"

There was talk of dreadful revenge but Kevin didn't care about persecuting Brian. The main thing he wanted was to make everything straight. "It doesn't matter now. He cheated and that's it. You'd better do your float instead!"

Joe couldn't believe his ears. "You're mad! Ours is in the official book! I'm still doin' ours!"

"Who with?" asked Kevin scornfully. "All your thousands of mates?!"

"What about all that work we done?"

Kevin could only remember the work *he'd* done, and now that Kevin had started a trend for fairness and honesty Danny didn't want to be left out. "It's not all settled yet anyway," she said. "If Brian cheated we have to pick again."

There was a general murmur of anxiety from the gang. There was so little time left now that the idea of wasting it arguing about what idea to do all over again made them despair.

Suzi and Liz started to think they had to go home for something, and they weren't the only ones, but Molly had been doing some quick thinking. "Hold on. I've got a better idea than that! Where's those fishing rods?"

They were just lying on the boat. Suzi passed them down to Molly – and Molly passed them to Kevin and Milo.

"First one to catch a fish! If it's Kevin we do the Battlestation – all of us! If it's Milo, we do Micro-wildlife."

Milo looked at Kevin, holding the red and gold Woolworth's rod he'd had since he was seven. "He's never caught anything in his life!"

Kevin looked at Milo, who held the same rod, bought at the same time, only in electric blue. "All he's ever caught is a cold!"

Molly was pleased. "Fish'll be in no danger then," she said, as the two hopeful anglers set off for the canal.

"It's true, that!" said Tessa to Molly, after the boys had gone out of the door. "Do you know just how hopeless at fishing they are?"

Molly knew.

In their first flush of enthusiasm, when they'd just bought their matching rods, Kevin and Milo had sat fishing by the bottom lock for ten days on the trot. They tried bread and worms, and maggots without so much as a nibble. In despair, Milo had fixed different coloured Smarties on his hook, but the fish must have preferred M and Ms.

They'd had lots of laughs though, and sitting together now on the same grassy bank watching the same floats not moving and the same fish not biting reminded them of those distant happy days.

After a long time of them both sitting in silence, watching some gulls circling overhead and some water boatmen skating over the still water, Milo spoke. "I don't really hate being called Milo."

"I know," said Kevin.

Another half an hour passed. The gulls flew off to Skegness for lunch. Some ducks came and ate the water boatmen.

"Do you think I'm a bighead sometimes?" enquired Kevin.

"Yeah," said Milo. "But it's not true what I said. They never used to call you Polly Parrotface in infant school."

"Oh, right!" exclaimed Kevin, with some relief. "What *did* they call me then?"

"Bighead," said Milo.

In the Boat Club Liz had been up to her arty tricks again. Everyone was gathered round admiring her latest drawing when Kevin and Milo came back from their fishing smiling all over their faces.

Kevin was ready to compromise. "Listen, everybody! Forget my idea! Let's do the Micro-wildlife Float! It's OK by me!"

Milo didn't want to be outdone. "No! We might as well join in with the Battlestation idea now! They've got the lorry an' the gear to do it up!"

Molly was pleased to see them like this. "Sounds like you caught plenty fish!"

"We didn't catch *any*," said Kevin.

"I mean – you're friends again."

"Sort of!" said Milo, not wanting to get sloppy about it, and then caught sight of Liz's new drawing. "What's this?"

"It's Liz's latest design for the float, something completely different!"

Milo couldn't see the sense in that. "We haven't got time to make something new!" But Kevin had the sketch in his hands and was looking at it with excitement. "Oh yes we have, Milo – it's *genius*!"

Liz smiled graciously. She was getting used to hearing that word.

Tea at Kevin's house that evening was a feast of peace pie and kindness pudding. Kevin and his cousins were gracious and charming with each other and everyone settled down afterwards to a game of Junior Trivial Pursuits, which Kevin's dad preferred because he could answer some of the questions.

However, just as the questions had been shuffled, the drinks poured and the peanuts emptied into the peanut bowl, this scene of domestic bliss was interrupted by the arrival of a well-known Committee spokesperson waving a well-known folder.

"They just can't do it!"

Nobody moved. Nobody offered a peanut.

"Can't do what?" asked Chris.

"They can't change the name of their float. It's in the official Carnival Programme now."

Lynda tried to stay calm. "I'm sure nobody'll mind."

153

Lorraine had lost any calm she ever had. "The Committee will mind. If it's been renamed it has to go back to the Committee, and there's no Committee before the Carnival – so that's that."

"That's what?" asked Chris.

"That's it!" said Lorraine with finality, slamming her folder on the table. "The float is unofficial and therefore illegible for a prize."

Chris thought she meant "ineligible". She did. "That's what I said! Ineligible! – *They can't have a medal*!"

Lynda picked Lorraine's folder off the table and weighed it in her hand. "Lorraine, who exactly is on this Committee that makes all these rules?"

"Well, there's myself of course and the Committee members."

"Who are?"

Lorraine's cheeks pinked slightly. "My husband –"

Lynda knew she was on to something. "And?"

Lorraine went from pink to red and flustered. "It's rather a small Committee."

Lynda thought she knew exactly how small. "Lorraine!" she said threateningly, "I think it's time you had a few more members! Don't you?"

It never rained on Mynstone Village Carnival Parade. In the fourteenth century, during a late summer storm the Sheriff of Mynstone had given shelter to a poor begger who turned out to be St Erik the Wheelwright. After drying out and revealing his identity he prophesied that it would "ne'er drop water on mun's head in Mynstone on that day hereafter, till the seas themselves do run dry".

They always held their fêtes on the feast of St Erik after that, and he'd never been proved wrong.

There was a special platform for the mayor and the dignitaries built outside the old "Sheriff's Hall", always by tradition without a canopy to show faith in Erik's prophecy. Here also stood the Committee members, who had grown from two to five in number and included Chris, Lynda, and the Captain, all sporting the same pink paper rosette.

They watched in enjoyment and anticipation as the first twenty-two floats trundled past. The Church Choir was on one, singing along with a tableau of St Erik in the thunderstorm, and the local fire service providing the rain. The Brownies were doing something unspeakably monstrous with a cardboard castle and a giant plant. The local dramatic society were chopping heads off with a guillotine and doing numbers from *Les Misérables*, without looking too unhappy about it. And there was plenty of flower-bedecked, noisy, brightly costumed ingenuity everywhere.

But only when number twenty-three rolled into sight did the crowd of spectators laugh out loud as well as cheer with approval – apart from Lorraine, that is, who stared with consternation at the complex spider-like metal space satellite on the back of Joe's dad's truck and the weird and brightly coloured giant humanoid garden creatures with space helmets over their antennae. She couldn't quite figure it out.

After the traditional three circuits of the church precinct it was time for parking up, scoffing and drinking and crowding round the platform to hear the Committee's decision.

Lorraine stood up, smoothed down her pink floral frock, tapped the microphone, made a very long speech which mentioned everyone, even some people who'd emigrated to Australia three years previously, and eventually got to the point.

"And so on behalf of all the Committee –"

Lynda smiled as Lorraine extended a hand in her direction – "I'm pleased to announce the winning float is Mynstone Brownies' 'House of Little Horrors'."

There was much enthusiasm for the Brownies' gold medal, and a big clap for the Choir as they picked up the silver. They were about to burst into a hymn version of "Shelter from The Storm", when Lorraine, to everyone's relief, interrupted them.

"This year, for the first time, the Committee have decided to make a special award – " Here Lorraine found it necessary to refer to a note she had just been passed by Lynda "– for 'stunning originality' to Mynstone Locks Boat Gang's 'Giant Alien Mutant Back Garden Creatures from Outerspace!' designed by Liz Collins!"

The applause was rapturous as Liz, a genius receiving her due, walked up to collect the medal looking not unlike a large greenfly.

It didn't matter about gold or silver. As far as the Boat Gang were concerned *they* had won, and they celebrated their victory with songs and cheers as they rode home all together, with Chris and Lynda and the Captain, on the back of Joe's dad's truck.

"Babs the Bun says 'We – have – won!'" chanted Molly waving her mascot in the air. This set everyone off again.

"We are the Car-niv-al Champ-yons!"

More cheers and more songs and then Joe called to his dad to stop the truck and the brakes went on so quickly that Chris nearly fell out of the back.

"What's up?" asked Lynda anxiously.

"It's the *Jezzy Belle*," explained Milo. "We're lettin' the Captain off."

Kevin and Milo helped the Captain down from the tailgate and then jumped onto the path beside her. Lynda called after them. "Where are you two going?"

"Fishing!" answered Kevin, causing a lot of laughter from the back of the truck.

"The Captain says we can ride back on the boat!" said Milo.

The truck started up. There were things Lynda wanted to remind them, but there wasn't time. "Don't be late!" she warned.

The evenings were beginning to draw in again, and the sun had sunk behind the parapet of the bridge as the *Jezzy Belle* chugged up the canal towards Kevin's house. Kevin and Milo stood at the tiller beside the Captain, still wearing their ladybird costumes, and carried on congratulating themselves.

"That's one of the best things we've ever done," declared Kevin.

Milo knew who should get most of the credit. "She's a genius, that Liz. Funny thing, though – she's hopeless at school."

"School doesn't always agree with geniuses," the Captain smiled knowingly.

"Yeah. That's true!" agreed Milo, with heartfelt sincerity.

Kevin looked ahead as the sun dipped under the bridge, silhouetting a darting flock of swallows, and let his thoughts wander. "New term'll be startin' soon."

Milo sighed. A deep thought was forming, but he was having trouble with the words. "It's been different this summer," he said eventually.

"It certainly has," said the Captain, who knew what he meant.

"Yeah," said Kevin, still watching the birds chasing their supper. "Shame it rained so much."

By the time the Captain had moored up and they'd said their goodnight the philosophical mood had passed. Milo and Kevin burst boisterously into the kitchen in their outfits, hoping to scare everyone and get a cheap laugh.

"Here come the Mutant Ladybugs!"

"Come to save you from the Evil Aphids!"

There were a few smiles but not quite the reception they'd expected. And then they took in the suitcases by the door, and the cousins all dressed and ready to go.

Kevin knew.

He'd just put it out of his mind, as he'd put Molly's arrival out of his mind the day she'd turned up at the door of the Boat Club.

"I told you not to be late," said Lynda.

"Where you off?" asked Kevin for something to say.

"Home," answered Danny for something to reply.

"I'm taking 'em in the van to meet their mother," said Chris.

158

"You just don't listen, Kevin," admonished his mum.

"It's OK," said Molly. "We'll see you again."

Everyone stood quietly waiting for something and then Chris looked at his watch. "Gotta go now or we'll be late."

Kevin grinned at Molly. "You wanna hand with your trunk?!"

"It's already on."

Danny picked up her suitcase. "The Carnival was brilliant!"

"Yeah!"

Kevin and Milo gave a thumbs-up of agreement. Lynda gave Danny and Molly a quick hug and decided on an upbeat goodbye.

"Off with you then! Bye-bye!"

This was the bit Kevin had wanted to avoid. Danny started towards the door. "Seeya then!"

Molly followed her. "Yeah, seeya!"

And then Kevin had an inspiration. He took Danny's hand and shook it, and then he shook Molly's hand, and Milo shook Danny's hand, and everyone shook everybody's hand, and laughed because it was silly, and because they felt better for doing it.

"Bye."

The door closed and they were gone.

The house seemed instantly quiet – and empty.

Milo and Kevin shared a look of sadness for a moment, and then Milo shrugged. "I expect they'll be back sometime."

Kevin pulled up a chair and sat in it as best he could with his cutaneous shell. "Yeah, worse luck!" And then, in a more serious tone to his mum, "They will be comin' back, won't they?"

"Certainly!" said Lynda confidently. "They wouldn't abandon such a dear old friend!"

Kevin and Milo followed Lynda's gaze to the middle of the table where, holding a toy fishing rod in her furry paws, sat Babs the Bun. There was a note on the end of the line. Milo read it.

"Babs the Bun says 'Keep having fun!'"

Kevin had to rub his eyes because the smoke had got in them from the *Jezzy Belle*'s engine.

"Huh!" he muttered, with as much despair as he could muster. "Girls!"